MW01378881

DADDY'S SEARCHING

PEPPER NORTH

Photography by FURIOUSFOTOG/GOLDENCZERMAK
Cover Model BRIAN NARANJO
Edited by CHERYL'S LITERARY CORNER

Pepper North
With a Wink Publishing, LLC

Text copyright© 2022 Pepper North
All Rights Reserved

AUTHOR'S NOTE:

The following story is completely fictional. The characters are all over the age of 18 and as adults choose to live their lives in an age play environment.

This is a series of books that can be read in any order. You may, however, choose to read them sequentially to enjoy the characters best. Subsequent books will feature characters that appear in previous novels as well as new faces.

You can contact me on
my Pepper North Facebook pages,
at www.4peppernorth.club
eMail at 4peppernorth@gmail.com
I'm experimenting with Instagram, Twitter, and Tiktok.
Come join me everywhere!

Dedicated to a very special Tinkerbell whose friendship I treasure!

PROLOGUE

"Belinda, please take a seat," Easton Edgewater invited, ushering me to a chair.

"Thanks, Easton. I'm intrigued by your request for a meeting today. What did you want to discuss?" Belinda asked, taking a seat and looking up at the powerful man who headed Edgewater Industries. She crossed her fingers. She wanted that cybersecurity job so much.

"I would like to offer you a promotion. I know you're interested in the cybersecurity position, but I'll be honest with you. Edgewater Industries needs you in a different position."

"If you're concerned about my knowledge, I can assure you I'm focused and dedicated to filling in any small gaps with research and courses," Belinda rushed to convince him.

"I have no doubt that you will be an expert in cybersecurity in a brief time. However, you are currently uniquely qualified to head up corporate technology. You know not only technology systems inside and out, you know Edgewater's network and the key employees. When I asked who the ideal candidate for this position would be, you were every single person's first choice. Not on their top five list or even top two. You were everyone's top choice."

"That's very flattering, but…"

"Belinda, you're not ready for the cybersecurity position. You haven't honed those skills yet. The leading expert in the field applied and has been hired," Easton said gently.

"The expert? Who, Pedro Morales?" Belinda joked. A picture of the magnetic, handsome man whose cutting-edge knowledge and experience overshadowed everyone popped into her mind. Something about his dark, swarthy looks and deep brown eyes did something to her insides in a totally unprofessional way.

"Yes."

Did he just say…

Belinda stared at Easton. Her legendary unflappability disappeared. She tried to gather herself and stop her rapidly quickening heart rate. "Did you say yes? Pedro Morales is joining Edgewater Industries as the next chief of cybersecurity?"

"He will arrive next week. Do you know him?" Easton probed.

Rocked by his answer, Belinda sat back in her chair. Pedro Morales was indeed the expert referred to in every cybersecurity article, journal, and class. Her hopes of being selected for her dream position evaporated in a puff of imaginary smoke. "You're not kidding."

"No. I'm not. As much as I value your dedication to the company, the opportunity to have Mr. Morales protect Edgewater Industries supersedes all other candidates."

Belinda nodded slowly. She strove to be at Morales' level in a few years, but Easton was right. The man would be an extraordinary addition to the company. "I understand."

"Your skills are perfectly tailored to become Edgewater's chief technology officer. Would you be interested in discussing my plans and my hope to have you lead that endeavor?" Easton asked, meeting her gaze directly.

Pushing aside her disappointment, Belinda focused on the opportunity he offered her. Before she'd heard of the cyber position, Belinda had worked tirelessly to distinguish herself in the tech department. It was a dream job as well.

"Of course, Easton. Technology is my life. Leading the department that I've helped build would be an honor."

CHAPTER 1

"Welcome to Edgewater Industries, Mr. Morales."

Pedro looked up to see a giant man behind the security desk. They seemed to have their own army for physical security. "Thank you. Call me Pedro. And you are..." He let his voice trail away purposefully.

"I'm Knox Miller. I'm in charge of security. It's nice to meet you, Pedro. Please call me Knox. Sharon asked me to watch for you this morning and smooth your way through the security processing for new employees."

"The royal treatment. Sharon is an amazing resource for Edgewater Industries," Pedro complimented.

"That she is," Knox confirmed. A glint in his eye clued Pedro in that perhaps there was some backstory he was missing.

"If you'll follow me to my office." Knox led the way to the security office. He opened the door by pressing his hand against the lighted panel.

Knox waved him to a chair in front of a modest-sized desk. The office was designed simply with only a few decorative touches. Pedro was confident that Knox paid more attention to his responsibilities than to his elevated position. As the powerful man logged into his computer, Pedro leaned forward to study the only personal item on Knox's desk—a photo of a smiling woman. It was a candid shot, not a professional one. Something inside of Pedro signaled to him that this woman was special. *Could she be a Little? No, that's not possible. Could there be more than one here?*

Knox set the ID card next to his blotter. "I'll need some information from you next. Driver's license and any other form of identification, please."

Intrigued to observe firsthand the procedures the company had set in place, Pedro unzipped the leather portfolio he carried and withdrew a passport and his driver's license. He handed them to Knox, who compared his likeness to both pictures despite already having recognized him upon Pedro's arrival from an unknown source. Knox scanned each into the computer on the desk before handing them back.

"Can I ask where Edgewater houses that information?" Pedro had already started his assessment of risks and weaknesses.

"Definitely. Each employee's personal information is stored on a separate server, which is not connected to anything."

"Just that computer?" Pedro followed up.

"There are two unlinked computers and a combined backup that is housed in an undisclosed location," Knox clarified. The twinkle in his eye clued Pedro in that Knox was a professional who'd already implemented basic cybersecurity procedures. Pedro was going to enjoy working here.

"So, if I tried to snatch the computer and run with it?" Pedro asked.

"Try it," Knox invited.

Pedro reached across the desk to lift the computer. It was securely bolted in place and the screen blacked out the moment he touched it. A thief could free it, but it would take time and wouldn't be quiet. An expert could bypass the screen blocker, but again, the expense of time and hacker expertise would be a hurdle. He nodded his approval.

"Where's the other computer?"

"In the main security office."

"You set this process in place?" Pedro asked.

"Belinda Jenkins and I did. She's the new head of technology, but a long-time Edgewater Industries employee. I look forward to working with you to fine tune anything we need to do better in security."

"Thank you, Knox. I have a feeling we'll have some long hours together."

Knox acknowledged the suggestion with a nod of his head. "I'll take a picture for your ID," Knox explained, gesturing at the footprints on the floor in front of a camera. "Before you ask, it's directly hooked to the computer as well, and the device itself doesn't store pictures in its memory."

Chuckling at the man's perceptiveness, Pedro stood and assumed the position. He smiled, aiming for a professional, yet remote expression. Quickly, Knox completed the photo.

Knox walked over to a small printer and scooped up the ID card as it dropped into the tray. "Almost done. They'll finish processing it as you complete your onboarding process. Ready to meet Sharon, who'll walk you through HR?"

"I'm looking forward to seeing her in person. She impressed me during our conversations," Pedro complimented.

"Let me walk you to her office." Knox gestured to the door.

Pedro collected his portfolio from the chair and walked back into the hall. They walked the short distance to a door labeled Sharon Ross, Corporate Headhunter. Knox followed him inside and handed Pedro's ID to the administrative assistant, who stood to greet them.

"Debbie, this is Pedro Morales. Pedro, looking forward to working with you," Knox said, extending his hand.

"Thank you, Knox. I'll be in touch," Pedro answered as he placed his hand in Knox's. There was no masculine aggression in Knox's handshake. No trying to out-squeeze him like some men would. Knox was confident in his strength and didn't need to prove it with silly games.

"Pedro." Sharon's door opened, and she emerged from her inner sanctum. "I'm so glad to meet you. Thank you... Knox."

Pedro noted the slight pause before she added Knox, as if that wasn't the usual name she used for the burly man. Immediately, Pedro connected the picture on Knox's desk with the lovely woman he'd spoken with several times on the phone. This just kept getting more interesting. Pedro watched their gazes meet and knew that glance exchanged a wealth of information. Without the picture, he wondered how long it would have taken him to put two and two together to figure out they were a couple.

"My pleasure, Roni." Light on his feet, Knox left almost silently.

"Please, come into my office," Sharon invited and led him to a comfortable seating area away from her desk, where two chairs sat next to a small table.

"Take a seat. We have an appointment in HR in fifteen minutes. Debbie will bring us some coffee," she said, glancing up at her admin standing in the doorway.

"I'd love some water if that's not too much work," Pedro requested.

"Of course. I'll take water, too, Debbie," she said before turning to Pedro. "Are you taking notes of all the cyber risks you've discovered already?"

"Nothing that's made me run out the door so far. The security protocols in place for dealing with the employees' data impressed me. Your head of security knows his stuff," Pedro complimented. There would be a million things he discovered that needed attention. Pointing out the positives as well usually kept people from being overwhelmed and discouraged. Balancing the psychological effects of change was one of the most challenging parts of his job.

"He does." Sharon's smile softened slightly.

Debbie interrupted with two bottles of chilled water and closed the door as she left them alone.

"Have you found somewhere to live?" Sharon asked. They had discussed housing on the Edgewater Industries' property in one of their phone conversations.

"I ran into a few snags in the move and just arrived last night. Everything is in storage at the moment, except for the things I'll need immediately. I'm currently at a hotel in town."

"It has been a whirlwind getting you here. Easton is expanding the single-family housing. I'll give you a tour of the campus when we finish here. I'm not sure if there is a house available now, but I know there is an apartment for you to use until they finish a home for you."

"I'd appreciate that. It's better to be close if something happens."

"That's exactly how our chief technology officer feels. She lives in the apartments as well."

"Sounds like our philosophies will mesh," Pedro observed.

"I have no doubt that you'll work well with Belinda Jenkins. She's the absolute best. You'll see her in a meeting this afternoon."

"Sounds like you have a busy day planned for me."

"Here's the schedule. If you're ready, we'll check off the second box and get all the miscellaneous paperwork finalized," Sharon suggested as she handed him a printed sheet of their schedule for the day.

Pedro appreciated her organization.

"I can't wait to meet Mr. Edgewater. His global design for this company is revolutionary in today's world," Pedro enthused. He'd done his research on Easton and his business before applying for the job.

"He's incredible. You have a meeting with him this afternoon."

AFTER A WHIRLWIND MORNING OF PAPERWORK, touring the campus, and meeting numerous Edgewater employees, Sharon ushered Pedro into the elevator for his most important meeting of the day. She had dedicated her day to getting him introduced to the company, and Pedro appreciated her time.

Sharon pressed the top button on the elevator display and leaned against the wall as the car rose. "I did check and there is not a house available at present. I've tagged you for the first choice when the next batch opens. In the meantime, I've reserved an apartment for you and had it stocked for you to move in this evening or tomorrow, whichever is easier for you."

"Thank you, Sharon. I'd love to settle in. I do have a cat, Tinkerbell. Will that be a problem?"

"Not at all. What brand of food do you feed her?"

9

"Him." Pedro laughed at her arched eyebrows. "It turns out I'm not an expert in determining the sex of a two-week-old kitten. I found him abandoned in the median of a highway."

"He'd been dumped?" Sharon asked, aghast.

"Yes. A car had already hit his sibling. I snarled traffic getting to him."

"Thank goodness. Tinkerbell is a lucky cat."

"He's a good boy," Pedro praised his best friend before sharing the brand and type of food he preferred.

When the doors opened, Sharon led him into a vast office with gorgeous views over the green space below.

"Pedro Morales, this is Piper, Easton's talented administrative assistant. If you need something and I'm not available, call Piper. She's an incredible resource," Sharon shared.

"She says that just because she hired me," Piper laughed as she stood to shake Pedro's hand. "But really, let me know if I can help in any way."

"I think almost everyone has arrived. Let me introduce you," Piper invited, leading them into the conference room.

"Pedro. Finally." Easton stood and walked forward to shake his hand. "Welcome to Edgewater Industries. We'll have some time to strategize later, but I thought you'd like to meet the heads of the departments I guessed you'd work with first. Take a seat."

Sharon sat in the empty chair next to Knox. Pedro smiled when he glimpsed the large man wrapping a hand over her thigh and squeezing a gentle hello under the cover of the table. They were definitely becoming his favorite couple. Sitting in the next chair, Pedro noted that one last chair next to him was empty.

"Hi, everyone! A server decided to go haywire at the last moment, of course."

Pedro stared at the newcomer. Belinda Jenkins. She was as gorgeous in person as she'd been on the Zoom call when he'd spoken for a cybersecurity conference. What had struck him most was not her beauty, but her thoughtful questions and the stuffie he'd spotted hidden behind her that peeked out between two ornate throw pillows. Delighted to meet her, Pedro stood to shake her hand.

"Mr. Morales, it's an honor to meet you. I heard you speak at..."

"Cybertron," Pedro added smoothly. "I remember. Belinda Jenkins, right?"

"Yes."

Pedro pulled out her chair, and they both sat down to join everyone gathered at the table. He heard a faint sigh of relief as she settled in her chair as if she'd been walking on those high heels too long for comfort.

"We're all here now. Let's get started," Easton said, drawing everyone's attention and eliminating any possibility of speaking with the fascinating woman next to him.

Forcing himself into business mode, Pedro opened his portfolio to take notes as Belinda twisted the lid on her cold bottle of water; Piper had provided one for everyone. Her arm brushed his lightly, and she whispered an apology.

Pedro smiled in response and dismissed her concern with a subtle shake of his head as he listened to his new boss welcoming everyone. Her delicate perfume wafted past his nostrils. He enjoyed the light scent that didn't overpower those around her.

"Oh, sorry," Belinda apologized again when a lock of her sleek blonde hair clung to his suit jacket. She quickly gathered her hair behind her. The hint of pink in her cheeks was endearing. The thought burst into his mind that he wanted to feel her silken tresses against his skin.

"Pedro, would you like to introduce yourself? I'm afraid I won't do you justice," Easton requested.

"Of course. I'm Pedro Morales. I've been involved with cybersecurity for many years, beginning in the military and progressing through my consulting business, serving a wide assortment of industries. After rambling around for a long time, I searched for the ideal company to call home. Edgewater Industries has been in my sights for a while. It is an innovative company in so many ways. Improving the company's resistance to possible cyber threats will help ensure that everyone here will be able to focus on helping achieve even greater success."

Nods echoed around the table as the powerful leaders of Edgewater Industries digested his carefully crafted words.

"Without firsthand knowledge of our systems here, what are the biggest global risks a company like Edgewater faces?" the chief financial officer asked.

"Speaking in general, phishing, ransomware, and crypto jacking are common types of attacks. These can shut a business down in a matter of minutes—sometimes seconds. Even more elaborate, cyber physical attacks like a takeover of a system regulated by technology, such as the air circulation system, could be deadly," Pedro answered bluntly.

Silence answered him until Belinda interrupted. "So far, we've been smart. We've paid attention to the best practices and have trained our staff members to be alert. Edgewater Industries employees are loyal and want the company to succeed."

"Thank you, Belinda. I have observed many positive established routines in effect today as I joined the Edgewater family. I look forward to working with each of you. Your insight and detailed information will help shape our future moves to guard the company from any vulnerabilities."

"I have asked everyone here to create space in their schedules to meet with you in the next week. I believe Sharon has set meetings up for you," Easton informed Pedro. He smiled as his carefully selected headhunter slid a sheet of paper in front of the newest employee.

CHAPTER 2

Belinda watched Sharon walk with Pedro Morales out of the conference room. She still couldn't believe she'd gotten to sit next to him. Now, if she could just trap him in a room somewhere and ask a million questions. Maybe a room with a pool so she could check to see if the rest of him was as muscular as the arm she'd bumped into. The corners of her mouth twitched up as she realized that was a bit creepy and possibly illegal.

"I'm glad to see you smiling," Piper whispered, sliding into Pedro's empty seat. The two women had become very close since Piper had become Easton's administrative assistant.

"I know you were worried I'd be disappointed I didn't land the cyber position... And I was for a short time. Then I stopped sulking and realized the opportunity it would be to learn from him directly, as well as taking an incredible leadership position in a company I love," Belinda confessed.

"That's my girl," Piper enthused. "So, did you know he was a hunk before today?"

"Maybe I need to rethink this new hire of mine." Easton's indulgent tone came from behind them and made both women spin to look at him.

Belinda laughed at Piper's flushed face. "Caught you, did he? That's what you get for objectifying the new employee. I would have thought you knew better than that."

"Belinda! Don't make it worse." Piper's embarrassed hue deepened.

"He is a very fit guy. I can see his military training and conditioning haven't evaporated completely," Easton commented.

"He competes in triathlons," Belinda mentioned casually.

When Piper and Easton looked at her questioningly, Belinda added quickly, "It's in his bio."

The Daddy and his Little looked at each other, exchanging a silent message that Belinda didn't need a written transcript to understand. They knew she'd checked him out with more than just a professional interest.

Belinda gathered up her things and pushed her chair back to stand. "Oops! Look at the time. I have a meeting starting in just a few minutes."

"See you for pizza tonight?" Piper asked before she could disappear through the door.

"I'll try," Belinda promised. Pizza night with the Littles was one of her favorite things about living in Tower B.

The remainder of the day went by quickly. There were a million items on her to-do list as the new technology head. It was late when Belinda finally called it a night and headed to her apartment. Pushing the large glass doors open on Tower B, she smiled at the gathering in the lobby.

"Pizza's on the way. Pete says they're two minutes out. Take a seat and wait with us," Alan invited.

"I should go up and change. These shoes are killing me," Belinda confessed.

"Take them off. We won't tell," Cynthia assured her. "Especially if you pretend not to notice the huge splotch of potato soup I splashed over myself first thing this morning."

"That soup was incredible," Sharon rushed to assure her.

"I had some, too," Tess commented. "I always look for the 'made by

16

Cynthia' sign next to one of the dishes before I choose what I want for lunch."

"You all are too nice. Thanks." She folded the fabric on her blouse over to conceal the large spot and held her finger up to her lips.

Laughing, Belinda dropped onto the cushion next to her. "I'm glad to sit down. These shoes are killers," she sighed.

Turning to Sharon, she asked, "Why aren't you at that gorgeous new house of yours?"

"Duh! Pizza! And Knox had one last thing to do tonight before we could head home," Sharon shared.

"Where is Knox?" Belinda asked, after looking around.

"He'll be here in a minute. He's helping our newest employee move into his apartment."

"Not Pedro Morales?" Belinda felt silly repeating his entire name, but only using his first name seemed too familiar for someone she'd been in awe of professionally. Like calling your beloved second grade teacher 'Doris' instead of Mrs. Butler.

"Yes. There's no single-family housing available right now. He's pleased to be able to stay on campus here with all the changes coming in the next few months," Sharon told her.

She looked past Belinda and nodded. "Here they come. I think Pedro's joining us for dinner. Knox was going to ask him."

Belinda watched the men chatting casually as they approached. Surely, the newcomer wouldn't recognize that many of the residents were Little. She crossed her fingers and breathed a sigh of relief that she was still in her professional clothes.

"Belinda, I'm glad you dragged yourself away from your desk," Knox greeted her with a smile before sitting down next to Sharon. He casually took her hand and rested it on one of his massive thighs. When their gaze met, Belinda could feel heat emanating from the couple.

"I found a good place to put everything on pause and came for pizza night. I couldn't miss that," Belinda answered with a smile. "Sit down, Pedro. Join the fun."

"Thanks." He sat down just a hair's breadth away from Belinda. "It's been a busy day."

"Where are you coming from?" Belinda asked, making small talk.

"The upper east coast. Nothing like this campus. Easton has created an incredible sense of community here. Like this." Pedro gestured around the room. "I'm picking up that the people here are from departments all over the company, just from their outfits."

Belinda followed his gaze. She'd never thought of it that way. Littles came in all shapes and sizes with a variety of talents and skills. "Living in the apartments jumbles us all up. I love having friends to run into all over the Edgewater campus. Alan's in maintenance. He's always glad to come fix a table or a squeaky door for me. Cynthia's food is remarkable. I thought Knox used to live in the lobby when I first moved in. He was always at that desk. Now, he has Sharon..." Belinda's voice trailed off. Was she revealing a secret? She looked quickly at Sharon to make sure she hadn't let the cat out of the bag.

"It's okay, Belinda. Pedro knows that Knox and I are together," Sharon told her. "Someone has a picture on his desk of me."

"Only observant people notice, and it's a beautiful photo of my favorite girl," Knox said.

Belinda couldn't help but smile at the perfectly matched couple. She knew some of their story. *Maybe someday, I'll find a love that strong.*

"Pizza's here!" Alan announced, interrupting the conversations around the room. Pete and another security guard walked in with stacks of the fragrant treat.

Everyone jumped to their feet to go nab a hot slice. Belinda waited for a few minutes to let the crowd disperse. When most people had retaken their seats, Knox stood and tugged Sharon to her feet.

"Let's go, Roni. I'm betting you missed lunch today."

"You'd lose that bet. I took Pedro to the cafeteria for lunch," Sharon corrected him with a wrinkle of her nose.

"I'm starving." Pedro stood as well. "I think we talked to more people during lunch than either of us had bites of the delicious soup Sharon steered me toward."

"Aha," Knox observed, hearing the other man's clue that perhaps Sharon had skipped most of lunch.

"Fine, feed me," Sharon said, throwing up her arms in mock exasperation.

Knox took her hand and escorted her toward the display of pizza delicacies.

"After you, Belinda." Pedro swept a hand in front to usher her ahead of him.

Belinda stood, instantly regretting her choice of stylish heels instead of comfortable shoes. She hesitated a minute before taking the first step. Damn, she wished she could take them off.

"Sit down," he requested and didn't seem surprised when she followed his direction without intending to. Before she could say anything, he squatted athletically before her and cupped one large hand around her calf, lifting it from the floor. The warmth of his touch sent a rush of desire through her as he eased the first stiletto from her foot before repeating the process on the other side.

"What are you doing?" she asked a bit too late, taken aback by his decisive action.

"Your feet hurt this afternoon when you arrived for the meeting. Those shoes are torture devices now," he guessed and waved a hand at the other discarded items sprinkled around the room. "I don't think anyone will care if you're comfortable, too."

"Do you notice everything?" she asked. Belinda didn't know what baffled her more—the fact that she'd just allowed him to take control so easily or that he'd noted earlier that she'd walked into the room gingerly.

"Something inside tells me to pay attention to you. I always heed those messages." With that enigmatic explanation, Pedro extended a hand to tug her to her feet. "Let's get some pizza."

Switching topics, Pedro talked casually about his day and the people he had met as they crossed the short distance. He pulled her into the conversation with insightful comments and questions.

Belinda struggled to pay attention to the conversation after his dominance and her immediate allowance of his care. She didn't understand her reaction. Why had she permitted his touch? When he placed a guiding hand on the small of her back to steer her around an employee who'd blocked their way, she found herself absolutely distracted. When they reached the display of pizza boxes, she stepped sideways away from him to give herself some breathing room. Surprised that she missed his touch instantly, Belinda struggled to regather her composure and dismiss the questions and fantasies whirling in her mind.

Grabbing the first thing she saw, Belinda tried not to blush as she handed him the hand sanitizer for him to use after touching her feet and shoes. "Would you like some of this?"

"Thanks for taking care of me, too," he answered with a smile as they both removed the germs that had accumulated over the day before picking up a plate.

"What's your favorite?" she asked, waving a hand toward the boxes.

"I'm a straightforward type. Pepperoni all the way," he shared.

"Too spicy for me. I think I'll grab these." She helped herself to a cheese and a veggie slice.

"Sorry," Regina said as she scooted in front of Belinda to grab a packet of dried red pepper.

"No problem," Belinda answered, automatically taking a step back to give her more room. She lost her balance as she bumped into the handsome man behind her. "Oops!"

"Careful," Pedro warned, wrapping his free arm around her waist to steady Belinda as she leaned against his hard frame.

"Good heavens. I'm usually not so clumsy," Belinda apologized as she stepped away as quickly as possible. The feel of his body against hers imprinted on her brain.

Stop it!, she scolded herself mentally. What was happening?

"I'm glad to help. Need any more pizza?" Pedro asked.

"No, I'm good. Shall we join that group? You haven't met everyone there," she suggested, noting that Sharon and Knox had moved to the larger gathering as well. There were two separate places to sit. She'd have some time to pull herself together.

"Sounds good."

He followed her to the large cluster of chairs and couches pushed together. A Little returned to take her seat, ruining Belinda's plan.

"There's room here!" Alan suggested, patting an open space next to him.

"Thanks!" Belinda said.

There was just enough room left in the last spot for her and Pedro to squeeze in together. Her thigh pressed against his hard muscles. *Don't think about it.*

Belinda took a bite of her pizza and chewed slowly, trying to look like she was following the conversation on the other side.

"Mmm! This is good," Pedro hummed his appreciation.

She closed her eyes to memorize that sound. Could he be any more appealing?

Thank goodness, the fun discussions around them kept her mind from wandering too much. Pedro was a skilled conversationalist and seemed to have a broad range of interests and knowledge. Following the pattern of the surrounding group, he stayed away from bringing up work-related questions or comments. Belinda liked that he had figured out that pizza night was for fun—not for talking about Edgewater Industries.

"Daddy had something fun happen to him today," Alan announced, after passing out bottled water to several people, including Belinda and Pedro.

Belinda crossed her fingers, hoping that Pedro had missed Alan's use of Daddy. From the corner of her eye, she caught his quick glance toward her. *Maybe he won't ask or know?* She forced herself to tune back into the conversation.

"What?" Cynthia asked, leaning forward to hear.

"We see a lot of interesting things at the gate. Today had to be my favorite," Pete shared. "A lady came for a job interview in the legal department. I asked for her ID when I didn't have her on the schedule. She didn't have one," he stated.

"She didn't have a driver's license?" Knox asked. His eyebrows pulled together in concern.

"No type of ID. No credit cards. Not even a phone."

"That's weird. So she was driving illegally," Alan pointed out.

"It gets stranger. She had a dummy in the seat next to her. Like one of those things at a store—a plastic mannequin. She'd dressed it like a man in a suit. As we waited for legal to get back to me and vouch that we should admit her for an interview, I asked her about it. It was her copilot so she could drive in the carpool lane," Pete explained.

"But she didn't have a license to drive?" Sharon asked.

"That didn't seem to stop her," Alan observed.

"No license, no ID of any kind, scamming the carpool lane, and here to apply for a job in the legal department?" Knox ticked the negatives off on his fingers.

"Turned out the legal department had turned down her request for a job interview after doing a background check on her. She had a fugitive warrant out for her. She'd escaped from a minimum-security prison two months ago."

Everyone's mouths had dropped open as they looked at Pete, except for Knox, who shook his head in resigned disbelief.

"What happened?" Sharon asked.

"The police arrived quickly," Alan assured them. "Daddy kept her occupied with questions while another guy called."

"Wait. She didn't have any IDs, but she had all this other stuff under her real name. Why didn't she use a fake name?" Belinda asked.

"Her law degree was under her real name," Pete informed them.

Everyone sat in stunned silence for a few seconds before Sharon piped up, "I'd like to point out that this wasn't anyone I found for the legal department."

The group dissolved into laughter.

"That makes my encounter with the soup a lot less splashy," Cynthia pointed out, making everyone groan at her play on words.

Belinda hid a yawn before dropping her crust on the plate. She never ate that part. "I'm going to have to call it a night. See you all tomorrow."

As she stood, Pedro joined her. "I'll call it an evening as well. Thank you for letting me join you," he told the group.

As everyone assured him he was welcome anytime, Belinda tossed her crusts and plate into the trashcan and retrieved her heels. She walked quickly to the elevator and called it. Maybe she could get upstairs before Pedro could finish chatting with the others. She didn't know what it was about him.

Just as the doors opened, he walked toward her. "Hold the elevator, please."

Pushing the button to keep the doors open, Belinda pasted on a smile. "Press your palm on the screen and it will take you to your floor," she explained.

"I think Knox set it up for me. Let's see," Pedro said as he followed her directions.

The door shut, sealing them in together. Pedro stationed himself against the wall by the panel as Belinda eased away to lean against the far side. She tried to ignore his magnetic presence, but it was hard as he looked at her. The silence was deafening inside the car.

When her floor appeared, Belinda positioned herself in front of the doors to make a quick escape. She stepped out into the hall as soon as they opened. Pedro followed her out.

"You don't need to walk me to my apartment. It's super safe here," Belinda assured him.

"I'm glad to hear that. I'm heading to my apartment. It's seven twelve."

Two apartments down from her? At least he wasn't right next door.

"It's strange there's no seven ten. Knox said something about the way they'd set up the apartments—some numbers are missing."

Belinda processed that she'd never gone past her door to check out the numbers. *That means he's right next door.*

As they approached her door, Belinda waved her shoes at him. "This is me. Enjoy your evening."

"I'll look forward to meeting with you soon. Sleep well, Belinda."

Stepping inside, she closed the door and leaned against the hard barrier. Belinda closed her eyes. She had to control her reaction to being close to him. Attending Pedro's lectures at a distance had mesmerized her. Being this close was dangerous. What was she going to do?

When no simple answer came to her, Belinda forced herself away from the wooden surface. *Shower and bed.* She wouldn't come up with a good solution tonight. Her mind was too blown.

CHAPTER 3

After tossing and turning for hours, Belinda had finally gotten some sleep. She groaned as she caught sight of the time on the digital clock. Dragging herself out of bed, she made a tall glass of iced coffee with a lot of sweetener and creamer.

"Oh, that's good," she said aloud to herself. "Maybe if I add some fresh air, I'll feel human."

Belinda pulled her robe snugly across her chest before letting herself out onto the small balcony of her room. She leaned against the railing and looked over the green space. "It's always so pretty here," she observed.

"Meow!" A soft sound caught her attention.

"Hi, pretty kitty."

The chatty cat rubbed on the inside of the railing as it answered.

"You are a good girl. Are you supposed to be out here?" Belinda wondered. The sliding glass door was ajar.

"Meow!" the cat assured her.

Enchanted by the fuzzy creature, she took another drink of her liquid caffeine and moved to the side of her balcony to study it. "You are very pretty," she complimented the creature.

"Thanks. I picked him out myself," Pedro assured her from the doorway.

Reaching one hand up to clench her robe closed, Belinda scanned his gorgeous frame, dressed only in a towel slung low around his hips. She forced her gaze up to meet his amused one. "Good morning. Sorry. She talked to me first."

"Tinkerbell is a great conversationalist," Pedro shared. "He's settled in the apartment already and decided he loved this balcony best."

"He makes quick choices." Belinda focused on the still chatting, petite white cat. "Wait, he? Tinkerbell?"

"Good thing I didn't decide to be a vet, huh? By the time an expert told me the girl kitty I thought I had was a boy, he already responded to Tinkerbell. He doesn't seem to mind it too much, though. Tink always knows when he has a good thing going. I say I picked him out, but Tink really chose me to rescue him. I was on my way to take a donation of toys and unopened treats and food to the local shelter after my previous cat passed away at the glorious age of nineteen. Turns out the same soupy treats that tempted an almost toothless cat to eat came in handy to convince the starving kitten by the highway to trust me."

"Tinkerbell sounds like a lucky kitty."

"He attached himself to me and started chattering like we were old friends. Of course, I couldn't leave him there," he admitted.

"How old is he?"

"He's seven this year. Lots of years ahead of him to enjoy the balcony or wherever we settle down."

Confident of their attention now, Tinkerbell fell silent and lifted a paw to his mouth to groom his luxurious whiskers.

"I'll let you and Tinkerbell enjoy the beautiful view," Belinda said quickly when Pedro stepped fully out of the doorway. *Does the man have no flaws?* She turned to scurry off the balcony.

"Don't run away because of us."

"Oh, no," she denied. "I have a lot of work to do this morning. I should get to my desk."

"All work and no play makes Belinda a dull girl," Pedro intoned wisely.

"But it makes Edgewater Industries a successful one," she countered, pausing to take a drink and watch his reaction to her words.

To her surprise, he didn't contradict her. He moved closer to lean against the railing that separated their balconies. Pedro nodded at the glass in her hand. "That's not good for you."

"I figured you were a health nut," popped out of her mouth before she could stifle herself.

"Because I work out?" Pedro asked, running his hand over his chest. "I've already revealed my secret weakness of pizza, but you haven't seen my weakness for my mother's tamales. Being healthy is important, but so is enjoying the good things in life."

"I'm glad to know you aren't a food tyrant. Just a drink one," she said with a laugh. "Ooh!" Belinda jumped when something warm and fuzzy rubbed against her leg.

"Tinkerbell! What are you doing over here?" Belinda questioned. She set down her glass before leaning down to ruffle the cat's fur as the small creature batted at her pink, fuzzy house shoes. At her touch, the cat flopped to roll on his back and purred loudly, inviting Belinda to pet his belly. After a few seconds of petting, Belinda picked the delicate cat up and cuddled him against her chest. "He's such a lover and so soft."

"Don't let him con you. He has a wild side and is an experienced escape artist. Bars and fences don't hold him back for very long. I'll put a barrier up so he can't get under the railing," Pedro promised.

"Maybe I could put it up on the far side of my space? That way, he could come over if he wanted to visit?" Belinda proposed spontaneously. She'd already fallen in love with the sweet boy.

"We can try that if you'd like. When he becomes a pest, just block him in to my area," Pedro suggested.

This time, at the sound of his voice, Tinkerbell twisted his body to look at his owner, one paw reaching out toward him.

"Looks like he's ready to go back to his daddy," Belinda said, reaching over the railing to hand him over. Instantly, Tinkerbell changed his mind and dug his claws into Belinda's thick robe, refusing to be separated from her.

"Rascal. Here, let me unhook his talons," Pedro said, immediately going to work to free Belinda without snagging her clothing. As he leaned over the rail, his towel caught on the railing and unwound itself.

She caught a quick glance of taut buns and gasped. Belinda immediately looked up at the clouds to keep herself from peeking. As Pedro held the cat steady so he could free Tinkerbell, Belinda felt his fingers brushing over the lapels of her robe. He didn't panic or release the cat, just continued to extract Tinkerbell's claws methodically from the material.

"Almost there," Pedro said reassuringly.

Belinda didn't know if he was talking to her or the cat. Her lips twitched upward, and she tried to keep herself from being amused. Who would have ever imagined that she could be this close to a naked Pedro Morales in public in her robe and fuzzy slippers?

"Are you laughing, Little girl?" Pedro said in that deep voice that sent shivers down her spine.

"N-no!" She tried to control the giggles that threatened to explode from her.

"Got him."

Automatically, Belinda looked down to see Tinkerbell curled up happily under the dynamic man's chin. When her eyes began to slide down his torso, Pedro commanded, "Eyes on mine, Little girl."

"Sorry!"

She slapped her hands over her eyes and peeked just a little as he set Tinkerbell down and picked up his towel. He wrapped it back around his waist and tucked it securely in place.

"You can look now," he assured her.

"Sorry..." Belinda had no idea what to say after that.

"I guess we have to be friends now, Belinda. I've seen your slippers and you've seen my..."

That was the final straw. Belinda lost it. When his low chuckles joined her delighted laughter, she looked at him and shook her head.

"I'm glad to have meet you, Pedro Morales. You're not what I thought you'd be like."

"That's a good start," he smiled.

"A start?" she questioned as she pulled herself together.

"Go get ready for your day, Little one," he instructed without answering her. "I'll see you soon. Comfortable shoes."

"Good idea," she agreed as she picked up her glass and walked back into her apartment.

Replaying their encounter as she ate a bowl of cereal, Belinda hoped she hadn't made a fool of herself. He'd seemed as amused by the turn of events as she had. Surely, he hadn't said Little girl and Little one deliberately, right? It wasn't possible that he was a Daddy. Not possible at all.

* * *

"THIS IS the server area for all the Edgewater Industries buildings. There is a dedicated team that is on call twenty-four/seven to maintain and protect access to these." Belinda forced the image of his naked buns from her mind for the millionth time and struggled to focus on equipping the expert with the knowledge he needed.

"You don't have any outside consultants involved in the infrastructure's management?" Pedro asked.

"We don't. Easton likes to have his own Edgewater staff in charge. Take your position, for example. Easton could have contracted with a large cybersecurity company with a ton of resources and an extensive knowledge depth. When I stepped into the chief technical officer's role, I did some number crunching and presented my findings to Easton for a variety of technology support systems. In the end, I agreed. It was a bit more expensive to maintain our own staff, but we have trusted employees who are dedicated to Edgewater Industries and trained in our system's features and quirks."

"How do you keep that team up to date with new technology?" Pedro asked.

"I have a training rotation. I keep my eyes open for new programs or roadblocks and the employees can submit areas they would like to expand their training. For example, on our server team, Mike recently received training for a new data warehousing system."

"Have you explored ways to protect the tech systems from cyber threats?" Pedro probed.

"I just stepped into my new role a month ago. At that time, I knew you were coming in to head the cybersecurity efforts. I've gathered some data for you but have put nothing into place."

"I'd love to see that data."

"I'll have my admin send it to yours. Do you have an admin yet?" Belinda asked.

Pedro looked at his watch. "I have ten minutes to make it back to my office for the first interview. Supposedly, someone named Fane picked out three candidates he recommended for the position. Do you know him?" Pedro asked with a piercing look.

"Fane's incredible. He worked his way up from the administrative assistants' pool to work with the second-in-command of Edgewater. If he recommended them, you're in expert hands," Belinda assured him.

"Send me that data if you would. I'll let you know my admin's name when I know it. Can I take you to dinner tonight?" he asked.

"Got more questions, huh?" she joked.

"No. I want to spend time with you," he answered directly.

"Really?" she squeaked before falling back on her professional persona. "I mean, do you think that's wise?"

"We'll figure that out. I'll knock on your door at six." His deep brown eyes held her gaze until she nodded.

"Thank you, Little girl. Six."

Belinda opened her mouth to ask if he needed her to walk him out of the warren created by the stacks in the server center but got sidetracked watching his toned derriere disappear down the aisle.

Stop looking at his butt!

Wait! Did he call me Little girl again?

CHAPTER 4

"No, this looks like I'm asking to be screwed," Belinda said to her reflection in the mirror. She looked at all the abandoned outfits on the bed and threw up her hands in exasperation before walking back into her closet to find something that would be perfect for a 'I don't know why we're going out to dinner, but I want to make the right impression' dinner.

When the doorbell rang, she dashed back out of her bedroom. She wasn't ready. Her hair! Trying to smooth her tresses after trying on a dozen outfits, Belinda walked quickly to the door. She peeked through the peephole to see Pedro Morales looking back at her.

Taking a deep breath, she opened the door. "Hi! I'm almost ready. Would you like to come inside?"

"You look lovely. Take your time. I brought this over to secure to your railing so Tinkerbell won't go past your balcony. You still okay with him coming to visit?" Pedro asked, holding up a clear piece of what looked like a thick plastic shield.

"I'd love it. Please do whatever will keep him safe. I'll be back in a minute."

Belinda hurried to the bathroom and heard Pedro open her sliding glass door. She tamed her hair and refreshed her makeup before picking up her shoes and bag from the bedroom. One last glance in the mirror made her shake her head. She'd have to do. It was too late to change again.

Emerging into the living space, Belinda found Pedro at her sliding glass door, looking out over the Edgewater campus. "It's beautiful, isn't it?" she asked.

"Easton has created quite an incredible place. I'm very happy to be here."

"After all the travel and lectures you've done, I'm sure you're tired of living out of a suitcase," she commented.

"Definitely. And Edgewater Industries had a special appeal for me," Pedro shared.

"Really? What was that?"

"Let's go to dinner and I'll tell you," Pedro suggested.

"Alright. Where are we going?"

"Knox clued me in to a special place to try. Are you up for a mystery date?" Pedro asked.

"That sounds like fun. Let's go for it." Belinda liked the thought of him checking with Knox for a recommendation. Pedro had planned this dinner. He wanted it to be a success.

She led the way to the front door and allowed Pedro to open it for her before hesitating. "I didn't even look to see what you did on the balcony."

"We can look at it when we come home. I locked your sliding door."

"Thanks. I never bother with that."

"Your safety is important, Belinda," he commented softly as he watched her close the apartment door securely before turning to join him in the hallway.

"Everyone has to go through security and I'm on the seventh floor. I think I'm well protected here. Not too many cat burglars on staff," she pointed out, leading him down to the elevator.

His responding low laugh sent a shiver down her spine. She felt his hand press against the small of her back as he stepped into place next to her. Belinda loved his old-fashioned manners. Heat radiated from that light touch, having a dangerous effect on her body as her nipples tightened inside her bra. She hoped the padding would disguise her arousal.

When the doors opened, she inhaled softly as she passed him and immediately regretted it. A hint of spicy cologne did nothing to mask his personal scent—earthy and masculine. Her arousal that had flared to life at his touch grew.

Help me not make a fool of myself, she thought.

Belinda settled against the far side of the elevator to give herself a bit of breathing room. Pedro selected the ground floor and leaned against the opposite wall. He scanned her outfit, doing crazy things to her heart rate as they stood in the quiet enclosure. The thirty-second trip felt like five minutes as she struggled to find something light to say to interrupt the sexual tension building between them.

"It's going to be okay, Little girl. I know it's risky because we haven't known each other for long, but you can trust me," Pedro assured her.

"Why do you keep calling me a Little girl?" burst from her lips.

"I'll need more time to address that. May I delay that conversation until later?"

He pushed away from the metal surface and walked toward her. The car shimmied slightly as it came to a stop. Belinda nodded to agree to his suggestion, feeling a connection—she didn't understand but couldn't deny—snap into place between them. When the doors opened, Pedro held out a hand for hers. "Let's go have a wonderful meal and get to know each other."

With a nod, Belinda intertwined her fingers with his. She allowed him to lead her into the large open space where the Littles had gathered the evening before. Waving at the guard on duty as they passed him, Belinda walked with Pedro out the door and to the parking lot.

A low-slung Italian sports car flashed its lights as they approached. Belinda ran her free hand over the shiny black paint. "This is yours?"

"I confess I have a weakness for powerful machines. I don't get to drive her often. Want to live on the wild side with me?"

"Only if you won't go at even half the potential speed this beauty could reach," Belinda joked.

She'd never ridden in such a fancy car. It both surprised her and didn't that Pedro owned this vehicle. He definitely made enough money to afford anything he wanted, but Pedro didn't seem like an adrenaline junkie.

"I assure you I would never risk your safety."

Pedro helped her into the vehicle and reached across her to fasten her seatbelt into place before closing the door. His assistance occurred so quickly and smoothly that Belinda didn't protest that she could do it. A flare of jealousy arose inside her.

How many women has he taken care of in this car?

She glared at him through the tinted windshield, sure that he couldn't see her. Schooling her expression as he slid inside, Belinda tried to push away her jealousy.

"How does the seat feel? You are my first passenger."

"What? That can't be right," Belinda protested, feeling guilty for scowling at him. How did he know what she was thinking?

"I assure you, you are the first to sit in that seat. My excursions are always solitary when I get to drive her."

"It feels good," she answered before steering the conversation into safer territory. "So tell me, what are your first impressions of our risk level?"

"Rule number one, no talking about work after hours unless it's an emergency," Pedro stated firmly.

"Number one? Will there be a lot of rules?" she teased.

"A few," he said noncommittally.

"Does that mean I get to set rules, too?" Belinda dared to ask.

"With my approval, yes."

"You're in charge?" she asked rebelliously, even as the desire inside her flared hotter because of his dominance.

"Daddies always take care of their Littles. It's their job. You need a break from all your responsibilities," Pedro answered in that deep voice that did things to her inside.

"What do you mean by Daddies?" Belinda asked, pretending that she'd never heard of that term.

"My gut tells me you know exactly what I'm talking about but are trying to hide who you truly are. I won't allow you to do that," Pedro stated evenly. "We are here, however, and I think you'd prefer to discuss this privately?"

He glanced over at her as he drove to the valet station. Belinda nodded her head vigorously. She definitely didn't want to talk about that in front of an audience.

Pedro circled the car to help Belinda step smoothly onto the pavement before handing his keys and a tip to the young man, who jumped immediately to get the chance to drive the stunning car.

"Be careful with it, please," Pedro requested as he placed a guiding hand at the small of Belinda's back.

"Of course, sir. This is the G.O.A.T. I'll take care of her."

"Thank you."

Belinda loved the smile of amusement on Pedro's face as they turned to the entrance. "Pretty spectacular to drive a car the valet thinks is the greatest of all time."

He winked at her as if it were an inside joke between them. "I would bet a few pictures will appear on that young man's social media sites tonight."

With his warm hand remaining pressed against the small of her back, Pedro escorted Belinda into the beautiful restaurant. She looked around in fascination. A meal at Les Trésors de la Mar had been on her bucket list since hearing Sharon describe how wonderful it was. The interior was gorgeous. She was super glad she'd abandoned those jeans on the bed and dressed up a bit more.

"Good evening, sir. Do you have a reservation?" the maître d' asked as they approached the podium.

"I do. Morales."

"Ah, Mr. Morales. Let me show you to your table."

In a flourish of elegant manners, he held out Belinda's chair and placed her napkin on her lap as Pedro sat next to her. Placing menus at their place settings, he informed them, "Your server tonight will be Jonathan. Enjoy your meal."

"I've never been here, Pedro. But I've heard wonderful things about it," Belinda leaned close to tell him.

"I have not either. We'll experience it together. Little girls are not usually allowed to drink but tonight is a special occasion. Do you like wine?"

"Red wine or sweet white wine," she answered as the waiter approached.

"Good evening. I'll be your server. I'm Jonathan. May I bring you anything to drink?"

"We'd both like water, please, and I'd like to see the wine list."

"Of course."

A few minutes later, Pedro lifted a glass of deep red Chianti toward Belinda. She grasped the thin stem of her glass and clinked hers against his. "What are we toasting?" she asked.

"To life's surprises," he suggested.

"I like that." Raising the glass to her lips, Belinda sipped the ruby liquid and smiled. "Ooh, I like that, too."

"I'm glad I chose wisely. Special occasions deserve special treats."

Before she could ask what the special occasion was, he gestured at his menu and asked, "What looks good?"

"It all looks magnificent. I didn't realize how hungry I was." Belinda scanned the menu. "Sharon always raves about the Steak Oscar, but I'm not a big steak fan. What are you thinking about having?"

"I am going to have exactly that. I think I'd have to wrestle Knox if I tried anything else," Pedro said with a laugh.

"No one should have to wrestle Knox." She scanned Pedro's body, remembering the powerful muscles that she'd spotted that morning in the infamous towel encounter. "You might be able to take him."

"No one should mess with Knox. I am looking forward to having someone to work out with though. Now, what is your first choice on the menu?"

Belinda's eyes flitted over the lobster mac and cheese. It sounded phenomenal, but the calories that had to be in that dish made her hesitate to order it. "I'll have a salad," she announced. That was probably better to have on a date, anyway. She looked up as the server approached.

"Our special tonight is the lobster mac and cheese. It is a delicious mixture of lobster, several cheeses, and fresh pasta. I highly recommend it."

Belinda fought herself. That sounded delicious. She glanced over at Pedro, who waited for her to order. "I'll have a salad…"

"We'll both start with a salad. What is your house dressing?" Pedro slid deftly into the conversation.

"We are known for our blue cheese, sir."

"I'll look forward to trying it. Belinda?"

"I like blue cheese."

"Perfect. And for the main course?" the waiter asked.

"The lady will have the special and I'll have the Steak Oscar, medium, please."

"Wonderful choices, sir, ma'am. I'll return with the salads and some bread."

"I was just going to have a salad," Belinda told Pedro quickly as the waiter left.

"I know. I also know that you wanted the lobster mac and cheese. If you dislike it, you don't have to eat it," he assured her.

"How did you know?"

"It isn't hard to read your body language, Belinda. Your gaze returned to that listing on the menu repeatedly and your eyes widened when he announced the special."

"You are very observant." Belinda didn't know whether it was spooky that he watched her so closely or incredibly flattering.

"Definitely when people are important. A treat is good for the heart and soul every once in a while."

"Thank you. I really wanted to try that." She took a sip of the delicious wine for courage before whispering, "Can you tell me now why you keep calling me Little girl?"

"How long have you known you were Little?" he asked gently, covering her hand on the white tablecloth.

"I don't know what you mean," Belinda said quickly, trying to control her surging pulse. He couldn't know, could he?

"Breathe, Belinda. It's okay. No one can hear us. How about if I go first?"

She nodded immediately.

"I've always known that I was different from other men. My desires are deeper and based on the need to care for someone in a very intimate way. I researched this feeling, reading and visiting adult clubs, just as I would investigate a new threat or weakness. Soon I knew I needed to be a Daddy for a very special Little girl." He leaned away and nodded at the approaching waiter to warn Belinda.

Mirroring his shift to sit straight, Belinda watched as the server placed a beautiful salad in front of her. Scattered with blue cheese and house-crafted croutons with just enough creamy dressing but not too much, the salad looked delectable. "This is so pretty. I don't want to eat it."

"Maybe if I take this crouton away," Pedro suggested as he stabbed one toasted bread cube with his unused fork, "it will ruin the image and you'll be able to eat it." He popped it in his mouth and chewed with obvious enjoyment.

"That's no fair. I love croutons," she protested.

"Help yourself," he offered, scooting his salad closer to her.

Without hesitating, Belinda pressed the tines of her fork into his chubbiest bread cube and ate it. "Yum!" she mumbled as she chewed. "Thanks."

"What's mine is yours, Little girl," he assured her.

Belinda took a bite of her delicious salad to give herself time to think. Pedro wasn't being pushy. He sounded completely sure. Did she give off some kind of 'I want to call you Daddy' vibes?

"Whatever that thought was, I'd love to hear it."

"No," burst from her lips before she realized what she was giving away.

"Why do you think I'm Little?" She forced herself to whisper the question floating around in her mind.

"It's not because you have something written on your face or the way you present yourself to the world," he assured her.

"Then how do you know?" she asked before automatically taking a bite of the salad in front of her.

"Have you ever looked at a display of desserts and known which would taste the best?"

"Of course. I always choose chocolate. That's my favorite."

"Exactly. Have you ever walked into an office filled with several people and known who you would click with as a friend?"

"Yes, but I know what kind of person matches my personality. Sometimes they fool you, but I think I'm an excellent judge of character," she added.

"Imagine if you've been searching for someone special for a long time," he suggested. "I've been a Daddy for as long as I can remember. I've developed a sense as well about people. Those I need to watch because they're dangerous or a risk, those who are dependable and honest, and those who are special."

"You think I'm one of the special ones?"

"I'm confident that you're special and I have a strong suspicion you're mine."

She stared at him, trying to control her expression and fearing he could read her mind. Finally, she admitted, "I don't know what to say."

"You don't need to say anything in particular. Eat. Enjoy your meal. I'd like to know more about you. Tell me, what's your favorite activity outside of work?"

Realizing that he was guiding the conversation to an easier subject for her, Belinda relaxed. After sipping her wine, she answered, "I don't have anything that I'm particularly fanatical about. I like lots of things from bike riding to reading. It depends on my mood and the day. What do you like to do other than work out?"

"My interests are varied like yours. Believe it or not, I went to the gym for the first time to work off the tummy I'd built up eating the bread I love to make," he confessed, patting his flat abdomen.

"You bake bread?" He looked like the type that existed on chicken breasts and vegetables.

"I'm an expert kneader," he assured her. "I discovered I enjoyed pushing myself physically. Searching for minuscule lines of code or tracing viruses back to the entry point is tedious to say the least. A little sweat helps burn off the tension from the day."

"I can see that. How did you get involved with cybersecurity in the first place or is that too close to the 'we can't talk about work outside of work' rule?" she teased.

"I think you're safe," Pedro answered with a smile in response to her light-hearted tone. "Believe it or not, I had a younger brother who loved to hack into systems for fun. He didn't have a malicious intent but simply enjoyed the challenge of trying to best the systems that others had set up. I spent a lot of time getting him out of messes."

"What would you do?"

"I'd fix the weak points he discovered to erase his tracks. I discovered that having a hacker search from the outside was a significantly more efficient method of checking for problems," Pedro explained. "I also learned to listen to my intuition. I have a knack for scanning code and finding problems."

The arrival of the server to remove their salad plates made Belinda sit up straight. Captivated by their open conversation, she had leaned in to listen carefully to his words. She'd never met someone as magnetic and interesting as Pedro. Having attended his conference lectures, Belinda knew he was a dynamic speaker in a large setting— one on one, he was mesmerizing.

She studied him secretly as the server captured his attention as he delivered the main courses. Pedro Morales was a handsome man— swarthy skin, deep brown eyes, shoulders a mile wide, and a powerful body that would put ninety-nine-point-nine percent of men to shame.

"Tell me if it's good," he requested, gesturing to the vat of melty cheese and lobster in front of her.

Dipping her fork through the golden-brown breadcrumbs on top, Belinda scooped up a bit of the steaming macaroni. As she lifted it to her mouth, his fingers wrapped around her wrist to stop her. Startled, she looked up at him in alarm.

"You'll burn your mouth. Blow on it," he ordered.

Automatically, she followed his directions, watching the steam swirl away with her breath. When it seemed safe, she placed it in her mouth. The scrumptious cheesy mixture was still very warm. It would have scorched her mouth if she hadn't given it time to cool slightly. As she enjoyed the flavor, Belinda poked a few holes into the topping to allow the steam to escape.

Looking up, she discovered Pedro watching her. "They definitely serve things piping hot here. Thank you for the warning."

"You're welcome. Is the flavor worth the danger of molten cheese and seafood?" he asked.

"Very. It's delicious. How's your steak?"

"Perfect. Just as I expected, Knox and Sharon know where to celebrate a special occasion."

"Are we celebrating?" she asked in surprise.

"Absolutely."

Not sure what to say, Belinda steered the conversation to less personal topics. "You've lived all over the US and abroad. What has been your favorite city?"

With a knowing smile, he answered her question. Pedro maintained the light tone of their discussions. Full of intriguing stories and facts, he was a perfect dinner companion. Belinda didn't know when she'd had a more entertaining meal.

"No more," she said regretfully as she set down her fork. Belinda couldn't eat another bite of the rich, cheesy dish.

"Looks like you have lunch for tomorrow," he suggested.

"Or dinner. I usually work through lunch. I need to clone myself to get everything done."

"That isn't healthy," Pedro told her with a frown.

"You don't need to worry about me, Daddy," she answered with a laugh.

Instantly, Pedro's hand covered hers and securely gripped it without hurting her. When she looked up to meet his gaze, he stressed, "That title is not a joke. Please do not use it again until you mean it."

He signaled the waiter. As the server approached, Pedro asked, "Would you like dessert this evening?"

"N-no. Thank you." Cursing herself for screwing everything up with a flippant answer, Belinda looked down at the dish in front of her. She'd just ruined everything.

The waiter removed her plate to box up the leftovers. Belinda knew she'd never eat them. Her heart was sick. How could she be so stupid? Trying to maintain her composure, she blinked away the tears that gathered in her eyes.

"Little girl, look at me."

Not quite in control of herself, Belinda held up a finger to ask him to wait as she dug in her purse for something important to buy herself some time. Finally, she pulled out her lip balm and rolled it over her lips before looking up at him. It gave her just a few seconds to compose her expression.

"Are you ready to go?" she asked, striving to keep her voice light and cheery.

"We'll be ready in a minute. The server is settling our bill. You are upset because I corrected your use of Daddy?"

"I'm not upset," she denied.

"That would be rule number two. No lying."

"All these rules and I've already messed everything up. I'll call for a ride home. I'm sorry. I hope we can work together professionally without allowing this to derail us." Belinda spoke quickly as she pulled out her phone to search for the ride share app she always used.

His hand covered her screen. "I will take you home, Belinda. Whatever happens between us, I will not allow it to affect our work interactions. This is going to be okay, Little girl. I promise."

CHAPTER 5

When the waiter returned, Pedro helped Belinda from her chair and collected the wrapped remains of her meal. He steered her to the entrance and signaled for his car. The valet raced to retrieve it, eager to drive the sports car again.

The ride home began quietly. After a few minutes, Pedro reached a hand over the console. Belinda stared at it, unsure what she should do. He waited patiently until she placed her palm against his. His fingers closed around hers and squeezed lightly.

"Everything is okay, Belinda," he assured her, glancing sideways to meet her gaze.

"I don't understand," she whispered.

"You've never been someone's Little girl, have you?"

"No. I've just read about it in books."

"That's why there are rules. Already, you have shared that you work an extraordinary number of hours and skip meals. While that is unavoidable sometimes when you have the responsibility you have at Edgewater Industries, it's not healthy. And lying damages any relationship—especially one as special as ours."

"I'm not a good liar. I try never to do it unless the truth would hurt someone's feelings," she confessed.

"That is an excellent policy to have," he complimented.

"Why did you come here? To Edgewater Industries? You could have a job anywhere. Why did you choose here?" Belinda held her breath when Pedro pulled into an empty parking lot and turned to face her.

"An inquisitive, bright student showed up on my screen one day during an online course. Her questions and her knowledge impressed me. More intriguing was the feeling I had that I needed to pay attention to her. I've learned in life to listen to that inner voice. It tells me important things."

"Are you talking about me?"

"Yes."

"You're saying that you came to Edgewater Industries for no other reason than to meet me?" Belinda looked at him in shock.

"I took a position here to work in an innovative company that searched for someone with my knowledge. Had you been working for a company that I did not believe in, I would have found another job as close to you as I could. I would have met you regardless of whether I came to Edgewater to work as your colleague."

"This is all very..." Her voice faded away as Belinda obviously searched for the word that would complete that statement.

"Surprising? Fortunate? Fated?" he proposed, feeling his lips curve into a fond smile. He wanted to make this all less confusing for her but couldn't. He could only support her as she reconciled everything in her brain. "I've had time to process my attraction to you and how I know inside that you are mine. You have not."

"Fated?" She echoed his last suggestion.

"I do believe in fate. Easton created an incredible business empire here. It was already on my radar before I encountered you. I know you are dedicated to our company."

"Our company," she echoed.

"Yes. I like what Easton is doing here. I would not work for a company that I didn't believe in. The fact that you are here is icing on the cake. I would have met you regardless of whether we worked at the same company."

"Because you think I'm your Little girl?" She repeated his earlier statement to double check she hadn't misunderstood.

"Because I know you're my Little." Pedro cupped her face, stroking her jawline with his thumb. "I know this is confusing and difficult to understand. How could I be sure that you're mine after interacting with you over a virtual call with a hundred other people?"

"How can you be so sure?" she asked.

"I don't know. Something in you called to me." Pedro leaned forward to press his lips against hers softly. When she froze under his kiss, Pedro lifted his mouth. He met her gaze squarely—not challenging, not forcing himself on her, just waiting.

* * *

A SMALL SOUND escaped from her lips as Belinda allowed herself to act impulsively. She pressed her lips to his and reached out to curl her fingers into the fine material of his shirt as he took control of the kiss. His mouth moved against hers as if she were the most precious person in the world. Tasting, tempting, the kisses lured her closer to his body. She unclipped the seatbelt holding her in place, only to find the console was a rigid barrier to her efforts to wiggle closer.

"Damn this small car," Pedro cursed against her mouth.

Laughter tumbled from her lips. Belinda loved that he was as frustrated by their location as she was.

"Oh, you delight me, Little girl. It's time for me to take you home. We will need to savor making love for the first time. This sporty car is incredible to drive but not so suited to pleasuring you."

He straightened her hair with a few strokes of his hand before reaching across her to drag the protective belt into place across her body. With his restored as well, Pedro shifted the car into drive and maneuvered the car through the evening traffic. His hand wrapped around her knee and squeezed slightly, as if he needed to touch her.

"You knew that was coming?" she asked a few minutes later after catching herself unconsciously tracing her lips with a shaking finger.

"I suspected that our connection would be combustible," he confirmed.

His hand stroked over the silky material covering her thigh. He did not make any moves to slide underneath, but her body reacted as if he touched her skin. She tried not to clench her thighs together to keep from cluing him in about the effect he had on her as she felt her panties becoming wet.

"It's okay, Little girl. My body also responds to you," he assured her softly as he pulled up to the guard shack at the entrance to the Edgewater campus.

She watched him reach behind the seat to grab a small blanket. He dropped it on his lap as he stopped. His motion drew her attention to the front of his trousers. Immediately, she blinked her eyes closed.

Surely not.

His chuckle assured her that her assessment had not been wrong. The arrival of the guard thankfully gave her a minute to regain her composure.

"Evening, Belinda. This must be Edgewater's newest employee. I'm Sebastien, Mr. Morales."

"Hi, Sebastien. Call me Pedro, please. It's nice to meet you."

"Welcome to Edgewater Industries, Pedro. Have a good evening," Sebastien said as he stepped back from the car to allow Pedro to drive through the gate.

"I like that there's a human on duty to make sure everyone is safe." He returned the blanket decorated with white paw tracks to the back and Belinda glanced behind him to find a small cat-sized cage filling the small storage spot.

"Tink always needs a blanket over his cage to comfort him when he rides behind me."

"I really am the first passenger in this seat?"

"Yes. Tink doesn't explore in the car. He's brave while the ground isn't moving, but while I'm driving, he's hiding."

Belinda struggled not to look back to see if her previous assessment had been correct. To distract herself, she played tour guide. "There are three towers and a variety of smaller buildings around the campus. Individual houses are located a short distance that way. There's plenty of space to expand."

"I will look forward to seeing Edgewater's future," Pedro said, pulling into a parking spot and turning off the car. He exited and rounded the back of the car to open her door.

Keeping her gaze glued to his face, she thanked him for his assistance. Pedro fell into step beside her. That warm hand settled on her lower back and steered her into the building. They stopped so she could introduce him to the new security man on duty at the desk before heading toward the elevator.

Standing in front of the metal doors, it felt awkward to know that they walked toward apartments right next to each other. When the elevator opened, she stepped in automatically and pressed the correct floor before moving to the side. Pedro followed suit but took a spot next to her.

The doors swished closed and he pulled her close to plant a fiery kiss on her lips. Pressed against his hard body, she wrapped her arms around his neck and clung to him for support. No barriers divided them now. Belinda reveled in the feel of his strength against her. There was no mistaking his body's reaction to her closeness. His arousal matched her own. When he stepped back, without thinking, she moved to follow him.

He gestured at the elevator door, which had opened without her noticing. Blushing, she turned blindly to walk out. Pedro's hand slid to her lower back to guide her down the hall.

At her apartment, Pedro turned her toward him and kissed her lightly before meeting her gaze directly with his deep brown eyes. "I've thrown a lot at you today. I have a feeling that the world seems a bit wonky tonight."

She nodded without meaning to as her thoughts jumbled in her mind. How had this man gone from her career idol to her colleague to her potential Daddy in just a few hours?

"I'm really sorry I called you Daddy like it was a joke. Do you forgive me?"

"Invite me inside, Little girl. I know what you need to feel better,"

Pedro instructed in a tone that did not allow her to refuse.

Belinda pressed her finger against the sensor and walked inside as he pushed the door open. "What…?"

"Little girls who try to deflect their emotions tumbling inside them need to learn how to express their feelings," Pedro told her, walking forward.

She stared at him in fascination. "How do you know what's happening inside me?"

"I don't know," he confessed. "There's a connection between us that grows stronger every moment we're together."

"So, how do I feel better?" she whispered, half afraid to ask and completely turned on by the man before her.

Pedro tugged the to-go container from her hand and set it on the entryway table. Then taking her hand, he led her to the couch. "Have you been spanked as an adult, Little girl?" he asked.

Staring at him with wide eyes, she repeated, "Spanked?" She watched him sit on the edge of the sofa and jumped back slightly when he patted his thighs.

"Lie over my lap, Belinda."

"I can't do that. We work together. How will I ever face you again?"

"At work we are professional colleagues," he acknowledged. "In our private time, we're exploring our connection that I'm sure tells me you're my Little girl and signals to you that you've found your Daddy. Can you be brave and let me prove to you that we're both right?"

As if she didn't have any control of her actions, Belinda found herself stepping forward to his side. His strong arms eased her into position, balanced over his heavily muscled thighs, just barely able to touch her fingertips and toes on the carpet. She was completely under his control. The feeling was both thrilling and terrifying.

His hand smoothed down her back and over the curves of her bottom. "Little girls regret their actions and need to have them wiped away so they can move on. Why I am punishing you for tonight?"

"I called you Daddy, trying to make light of our conversation, because I was scared," she admitted, staring at the flooring below her. It was easier to tell the truth when she didn't have to look at him.

"Good girl." Pedro lifted her skirt and smoothed it over her back.

When she jumped in reaction, he explained, "Little girls always get spanked on their bare bottoms. If there is something between your skin and mine, the bad feelings don't disappear completely."

"That's embarrassing," she whispered, trying to staunch her body's reaction to the thought of Pedro seeing her so intimately. Her panties were already soaked. He'd know. Belinda couldn't believe that she was allowing him to touch her like this. She worried she'd never be able to look at him again.

"There are no secrets between a Daddy and his Little girl."

The statement rang completely true in her mind. He was right. Belinda bit her bottom lip as she felt his fingers guide her lacy panties over her hips to encircle her thighs.

The first swat drew a gasp from her lips. The sting captured her attention. Quickly followed by another, Belinda felt his hand land on different spots across her sensitive skin, keeping her off balance, heating her bottom, and making her wiggle on his lap. Only able to concentrate on the sensations filling her mind, Belinda's embarrassment faded from her mind as tears filled her eyes.

"I'm sorry. I'm so sorry," she wailed as suddenly all the tension fled from her body and she submitted fully to his control. "I'll never use Daddy as a joke to cover up what I'm really feeling. I was so scared, I didn't know what to say."

Her punishment stopped immediately. Pedro lifted her to sit on his lap. Her fiery bottom pressed into the corded muscles of his hard thighs covered by his smooth wool suit, the prickly feeling continually reminding her of his discipline. Belinda pressed her face into the curve of his throat as he rocked her gently.

"What could you have done differently?" he asked quietly.

"I could have just told you I was scared," she mumbled against his skin.

"Daddies specialize in helping their Little girls feel more secure. That helps with that scared feeling."

"How?"

"Maybe you needed to know that I respect your skills and knowledge. That I will never undermine you or take away the control you've earned at Edgewater Industries. You're my Little girl. I want to see you continue to excel. I'm here to support you if I can."

"I still get to be the professional me at work?"

"No one who cares about you would ever jeopardize that," he assured her.

"My Daddy wouldn't," she agreed, peeking up to meet his gaze.

"Your Daddy certainly wouldn't," he agreed. "You're safe with me, Little girl."

"Where do we go from here?" she asked.

"You go to bed and sleep like a baby, knowing that all the bad stuff you worried about is gone now. I'd like to hold you close all night but I want you to be as sure as I am that you are my Little girl before we take that big step. Only then will I take you to bed."

Belinda nodded as she squeezed her legs together. She was more turned on than she'd ever been but she wasn't ready. And he didn't know all her secrets.

His hands wrapped around her waist and he lifted her to her feet. Pedro slid her panties down to the floor and helped her step out of them without any awkwardness before standing and wrapping his arms around her. His mouth captured her lips with a sweet kiss that almost hid his desire for her. She liked that he struggled to hold himself under such rigid control.

"Put your lunch in the refrigerator." He reminded her of the leftovers as he led her back to the door.

"It will all be okay," he reassured her before adding, "Sleep well, Little girl." Pedro blew her a kiss as he backed down the hallway toward his apartment. He did not enter his apartment until she was safely inside hers.

Shaking her head as she locked the door behind her, Belinda stashed the macaroni in the fridge before turning off the lights. Deciding fresh air might calm her thoughts, Belinda opened the balcony door a few inches and leaned against it as she breathed in the cool night breezes. A swishing tail flicked her leg as the fluffy cat waltzed into her apartment.

"Tinkerbell. You should go home. It's late," Belinda told him.

With a meow, the creature turned and disappeared into the darkness of her apartment. Belinda called him several times, but the cat did not respond. Exhaustion crashed over her. She decided to go shower, guessing that Tinkerbell would be ready to stop exploring her apartment by then, and she could let him back out again. She closed and locked the door.

Twenty minutes later, Belinda had looked and called for that silly cat. Not finding him immediately, she gave into her exhaustion and turned out the lights to crawl into bed. Turning onto her stomach, Belinda slid her arm under the pillow and closed her eyes. The bed dipped slightly and a warm body settled against the curve of her body.

"Tinkerbell," Belinda reproached. The cat simply cuddled a bit closer to her.

Belinda considered getting up to put the purring feline on the balcony so Tink could make his way to Pedro's apartment, but the silly cat seemed happy to sleep with her. Closing her eyes, she cascaded into sleep.

CHAPTER 6

"Meow?"

Belinda blinked her eyes open at the sound and looked straight into a pair of green eyes. "Hi, Tinkerbell. Did you sleep well?"

The cat rubbed his face against Belinda's nose in response and began purring.

"I'll take that for a yes," Belinda answered with a laugh. "Are you ready to go home?"

Tinkerbell turned and swished his tail regally before jumping off the edge of the bed to land silently on the carpeted floor.

Belinda pushed herself up to sit on the edge of the bed and yawned before getting up. Rubbing a hand through her tousled hair, she followed her evening visitor through the apartment to the balcony door. When she opened it, Tinkerbell waltzed out and turned to meow his thanks before heading toward Pedro's apartment.

Curious to watch the cat navigate from one balcony to the next, Belinda leaned out and froze.

"Good morning, Little girl. Come out and join me," Pedro invited. He held a steaming cup of coffee in his hand.

Belinda tried to focus on his face but failed miserably. The allure of his rock-hard body dressed only in low-slung pajama bottoms was too much to resist. *Damn!* At his chuckle, she realized she had stared for way too long and that she probably looked like a mess. Her hands immediately flew to her hair and she tried to smooth her rumpled locks into place.

"You look adorable, Little one. Come out and chat. I'll share my coffee," he offered. "How is your bottom?"

"Sore." Belinda focused on the railing between them, unable to meet his gaze.

"And your mind?" he probed.

"Better," she admitted. "I slept really well."

"I'm glad."

Walking forward slowly, she attempted to fill the silence that followed. "I should have sent you a message that Tinkerbell was with me," Belinda apologized.

"No need. I watched him dart into your apartment and knew he planned to snuggle with you last night. I was understandably jealous," he admitted as he offered her the handle of the large cup.

Automatically, she accepted it and took a sip of the dark, rich coffee. "Mmm! This is amazing. This isn't the normal coffee stocked in these apartments."

"It is my own special blend. You have found the first of my faults. I am a coffee snob," Pedro confessed.

"The first of your faults," she echoed, unable to hide her curiosity.

"I also suddenly find myself possessive and protective."

The heated look he gave her left no doubt in her mind that he referred to her as the object of his attention. She looked down at the cup and took another sip to give herself time to think.

"Have you had a Little girl before?" she blurted, darting a look up at his face to judge his reaction. To her surprise, he didn't look guilty, but sad.

"I have. Do you want to hear about her?" Pedro asked softly.

"I don't want to, but I think I need to," she confessed.

"Elizabeth was my first love. Not a schoolboy romance as I was already in my twenties. It was, however, the first time I thought I'd found the woman suited for my desires. She was shy and enjoyed being at home. I met her while investigating a break-in for a major insurance company. An actuary, numbers and risk assessments ruled her life. I wooed her for six months before discovering she was the source of the security risk."

"Was she really Little?"

"She was. Unfortunately, she needed a different type of Daddy. The shy demeanor covered her deft manipulations and misdeeds. I couldn't trust her," Pedro admitted, shaking his head. "Our relationship shook me to my core. I didn't date for two years after that."

"Do you think you've ever gotten over it?" she asked.

"Oh, yes. I was more angry at myself for being deceived than I was angry she'd hoodwinked me."

"She was your only Little?"

"My only serious relationship. I have played with Littles at BDSM clubs. There was never anything serious between them and me. Then I met you. I told myself that you couldn't be as perfect as you appeared. I was wrong."

"I'm not perfect," she laughed.

"You are perfectly you. I don't want you to be anyone else. Now, you..."

The beeping of her alarm sounded faintly from her room. "Sorry. I have to go. Maybe I'll see you at work."

Belinda fled into her apartment and flipped the lock on the balcony door. Running to her bathroom, she splashed her face with water and tried to pull herself together. Twenty minutes later, she let herself out the door and closed it quietly. Dashing to the elevator, she mentally pleaded with it to open fast. When the metal doors closed behind her, there was no sign of Pedro.

Once in her office, Belinda logged into her computer and checked her schedule. She had a variety of meetings and conferences. In her previous position, Belinda had worked with almost all the division leaders. Now, she was holding a series of meetings with each department to assess their technology needs. The first session scheduled for today was in forty minutes in Tower C. She blinked and looked back at the computer. Pedro Morales was listed as an attendee.

Glancing down the rest of her daily schedule, she noted his name at every single meeting. This was too much. Had he done this before or after assuring her that he wasn't going to challenge her authority? She pulled up the ABC Towers employee list to locate Pedro's phone number. It wasn't listed. Belinda rolled her eyes in aggravation.

She called HR. They had done the hiring. They had to have his number or his office location. In a minute, she had both pieces of information.

His office was down the hall from her on the sixth floor of Tower C. Grabbing her tablet and phone, Belinda headed for the elevator. She stewed as she waited. How dare he waltz into her schedule without asking! The thought that he might undermine her authority as the head of technology rebounded into her thoughts. She'd worked too hard at Edgewater Industries. Belinda didn't care how world famous he was.

Plastering a friendly smile on her face when the elevator opened, Belinda hid her emotions from her colleagues as they greeted her. She maintained her congenial demeanor as she waved and bypassed his admin to rap on his door.

"Belinda! Hi!" Pedro stood and rounded his desk to greet her.

"I'm going to shut this door if that's okay?" she spit through her teeth.

"Of course." He led the way to a small conversation area at the side of his large office.

Belinda closed the door with a deliberately quiet click. She stalked forward and stood an arm's distance from him. "Why are you at every meeting I have today? Was everything that happened last night a complete lie?"

"Nothing that happens between us is a lie. I looked at that schedule this morning and was surprised as well. I don't know how this happened without your knowledge." Pedro spoke precisely and gently.

"No one called, messaged, or emailed. I watched it appear on my schedule this morning," she answered, hearing the clipped tone marking her words. She was pissed.

Pulling out his phone, Pedro selected a number just as a knock sounded on the door. They both could hear the ringtone on the other side of the barrier.

"Hello? Pedro? I'm at your door. Could I talk to you?" Sharon's voice was easily recognizable.

He looked at Belinda and answered, "Please come join us, Sharon."

"Crap! I didn't get to you fast enough."

"Belinda came to speak with me when she noticed my name appearing on the schedule for each of her meetings today," Pedro explained.

"I should have taken care of it myself," Sharon quickly shared. "I put Pedro's schedule for the next week together myself, Belinda. When I spoke to the head of accounting, he mentioned you were coming in today to speak to him. He asked if he could meet with both of you for a longer time since he felt there was a connection between technology and cybersecurity needs."

Belinda nodded as the new corporate headhunter paused. She glanced over at Pedro.

"I emailed asking you to let me know if you could see any negative aspects of a joint meeting. I didn't hear anything back, so I figured that you agreed," Sharon added quickly.

"I did not receive a message, Sharon." Belinda's tone was professional, but curt.

"I know. It's my fault. Instead of emailing last week, I included it with the scheduling addition. I expected it to be effective days ago so you could react. When I logged in this morning, I discovered a notification that the system had delivered the email today and updated Pedro's schedule in one vast sweep—also today twenty minutes ago," Sharon explained.

"The scheduling system has a section to send prior notification, but that is only possible on the advanced settings screen," Belinda provided. "I've had others complain messages sent through the scheduling system are not received until the last moment."

"Email is best sent through the email system," Belinda added.

"I've learned my lesson," Sharon said, raising her hand as if swearing an oath. "I am so sorry for any confusion. Do you want me to remove them and schedule Pedro separately?"

Belinda looked at her, trying to keep her frustration from showing on her face. There was no way to refuse with Pedro standing at her side. "No. It's already on everyone's schedule. I have meetings all week..."

"I'll reschedule the ones in the future myself," Sharon assured her quickly.

Belinda pulled her schedule up on her tablet and blinked. Sharon had scheduled Pedro in every single meeting she had. What the...

"Sharon, I think Belinda and I need to talk privately to develop a strategy to make the most of this situation. I will call you with our decision for the future meetings," Pedro interjected smoothly. He escorted Sharon from the room and closed the door once again.

"My apologies, Belinda. I understand how this must have looked to you."

"I may not be the director of cybersecurity, but I have excelled in all my positions at Edgewater Industries and was chosen to lead the technology department." Belinda established her credentials with a steely look. She was not backing down. Even if he was the yummiest specimen of man flesh she'd ever met and stood in front of her and claiming to be her Daddy.

"Exactly. My job has a fancy title and is on the firing line if something happens. Your job ensures that Edgewater Industries functions on all levels and at all times. We have fifteen minutes before we need to leave for your first meeting. Let's figure out how to make this work." Pedro waved her into a chair. He jogged to his desk and grabbed an old-fashioned notepad and a pen before joining her.

Pulling up her checklist of items she had established when scheduling these meetings, Belinda looked at the time frame she had estimated and divided it by half. She shook her head. There was no way to accomplish her goals in such a limited time frame.

"This is your meeting. How much time did you allot for the division leader to ask questions?" Pedro asked.

"Ten minutes of each hour-long meeting," she snapped. Belinda didn't wish to give up that time. Their questions would tell her information she needed to know about lack of communication or training.

"The people you're meeting with have met you?" he asked.

"Yes."

"Could you take one minute to introduce me and then move on to your plan?" Pedro suggested. "I'll use part of that minute to state that I'm joining you simply to meet everyone, be time efficient, and gather overlapping information between our two departments."

"And you're going to be quiet for the rest of the time?" she scoffed.

"Watch it, Little girl. I know you're angry, but remember, I did not cause this situation."

"I am not a Little girl at work," she hissed.

"You're a Little girl all the time," he corrected her with the first stern look she'd received since closing the door to talk to him. "I will make notes and only ask questions if there is a dead space of time."

Belinda rolled her eyes. *Sure he would.*

"Can I see your list of topics?" he asked.

She handed it to him silently, waiting for him to criticize something.

"Perfect. I would ask several of those questions myself. If time allows, I will ask this question, 'what security gap have you found or worry about?'"

"That's it?"

"That's it," he confirmed. "As we move from meeting to meeting, I could benefit from your knowledge of the person next on your schedule."

Somewhere in a small segment of Belinda's attention, she noticed that he always referred to these as her meetings, her schedule, and her agenda. She wasn't ready to trust him yet. As her mom always said, 'The proof's in the pudding.' That first meeting would tell her all she needed to know.

"It's time to leave," she snapped.

"Let's go."

Pedro preceded her to the door and opened it. Gallantly ushering her through, he joined her at the elevator when she didn't pause so he could walk with her. They stepped into the car and when it started down, she tried to relax the tension building between her shoulder blades. She glanced down at her notes and gathered her thoughts.

When they reached the fourth floor, she stepped confidently out of the elevator and paused for Pedro to join her. As they walked through the floor Belinda had worked on for years, many employees looked up from their cubicles to wave and call hello. She was equally pleased to see them as well. Belinda would have remained there, but she knew Easton was correct in stationing the chiefs of the department on a different floor. She would be less efficient if people could just drop in to see her. There were others in charge of the jobs she'd held before. She needed to let them do their work without interference.

"Belinda, I've been looking forward to our meeting," John commented as he welcomed the duo into his office. He smiled at the man behind her.

"Thank you for your time, John. This is Pedro Morales. He's the new chief of cybersecurity. As you can imagine, there's an overlap between overall technology at Edgewater and cybersecurity. We decided it would be most efficient of your time if we met with you together. Mr. Morales will schedule further meetings with you as needed," Belinda said smoothly, keeping her emotions from showing on her face.

"Nice to meet you, John," Pedro said and shook the man's hand. "This is Belinda's meeting. I'm just eavesdropping."

"I'm glad you could join us. Please take a seat." John waved a hand at the chairs in front of his desk.

Immediately, Belinda guided the conversation through all the topics she wished to discuss for the meeting. She noticed Pedro making notes on his pad of paper as she jotted items to remember on her tablet. Pleased with the progress by the end, Belinda opened the conversation up to John's questions.

He asked several questions about funding and supply issues before glancing at Pedro. "May I ask you what you're looking for?"

Pedro glanced at Belinda and asked, "Do you have anything else you'd like to follow up on first?"

When she shook her head, Pedro continued, "Every company has their own challenges. It could be something as confounding as employees who open risky emails or something as complex as a coding error that may have been around for years. I'll dive into everything but would love to know your greatest cybersecurity concern."

"To be honest, the newest computers coming in are scary fast. That's great for time efficiency, but I wonder how many employees are clicking on random messages that pop up without taking the time to read them completely. I'll give you an example that happened to me. I was in the middle of saving a spreadsheet for the monthly budget. Normally a message pops up to ask if I wish to leave the application after I've finished saving. I almost clicked it automatically, but the word accessible caught my eye. When I stopped to read it completely, the computer was asking for permission to make this file accessible to various people in the department. Probing deeper, I found a name I didn't recognize. It was a consultant who'd installed our virus system on the new laptop I'd just been given."

"I remember you reporting that last week. We implemented a new policy to remove permissions granted to a contractor before we assign a computer to an Edgewater employee. In addition, all the computers that consultant worked on were recalled and extraneous names were removed," Belinda commented.

"I knew you'd taken care of it thoroughly," John confirmed. "It got me thinking, if I hadn't noticed and dug, would anyone else have? Many departments are working overtime. Would someone have taken the time I did to check something out or report it? Or would they have been too busy?"

"Unfortunately, that rushed click is often how a hacker gets inside. They could target a million employees at a million different companies to try to get one person to grant them access. Thank you, John, for suggesting processing messages as a target to lock down. It sounds like you, Belinda, and the technicians handled the situation perfectly."

"Yes. I was very pleased with the response my concern was given. It definitely opened my eyes to threats I hadn't considered. While I've got you here, Belinda, let me ask you..." John opened his laptop and accessed a list of questions he'd created before the meeting. Quickly, he addressed the remaining items on his list and jotted notes.

When Belinda and Pedro stood to leave, John followed them to the doorway. "Thank you for meeting with me. I appreciated an update on the plans for technology in general and a taste of what cybersecurity will address."

"Our pleasure, John. Thank you for your time," Belinda said as she stepped into the hallway and advanced a few steps for Pedro to exit and join her.

"So, do you think there are any advantages for you to continue to tag along?" Belinda asked.

"Yes. Other than the obvious issue that you dealt with efficiently, I also picked up on several other risk factors. He started his computer without using any login or biometrics like his fingerprint. Anyone could have pulled up his files if the rest of it was unprotected."

Belinda turned her notes to show him she'd jotted down the same idea. "Great minds," she said sarcastically.

When they stepped into the empty elevator to descend to the ground floor, Pedro warned, "Enough, Little girl. We need to work together."

"What are you going to do? Spank me again?" Belinda laughed, feeling like a fool.

"I understood your reaction to these combined meetings. I would have been angry as well to see a newcomer's name pop up in my meetings. We've figured out how to make this a positive rather than a negative. Enough with being deliberately confrontational."

He held her gaze for several long seconds before adding, "And yes."

The door opened before she could respond. By the time they'd finished the last morning meeting, Belinda's anger had dissipated completely. Pedro was allowing her to run her meetings and only asking questions if time allowed. Part of her wanted to stay snarly. *Of course he's playing nice. I made him.* The other half realized he wasn't responsible for the mistake and had taken steps to create a positive result. *And I've learned important things as well today.*

Pedro excused himself at lunchtime to visit the human relations department. They had urgent paperwork for him to complete. Belinda ate a solitary meal at her desk and had to admit she missed him.

CHAPTER 7

"We need to discuss today," Pedro told her quietly as they walked back to Tower C after their last meeting.

"I'm afraid I have some work to do to get caught up from being out of my office all day," Belinda said quickly. She wasn't ready to talk yet.

"If you promise me our conversation will take place soon, I'll give you some alone time," Pedro suggested.

She stared at him. "You always know what I'm thinking."

"I'm glad. That makes it harder for you to hide from me. Now, do I have your promise that we'll talk later tonight?"

When she nodded, he said, "Then I'll go to check out the gym this evening, Knox invited me to join him earlier. He's going to kick my butt. I haven't been to the gym in a while."

"I'll get notes typed up while it's fresh in my mind," she shared, forcing a picture of Pedro's muscles rippling as he lifted weights out of her mind.

"We will talk soon," Pedro promised, capturing her gaze.

"Soon," she echoed, before turning to disappear into her office. She held her breath, hoping he would continue down the hallway. Belinda heard silence for a few seconds and then footsteps that faded away.

Forcing herself to focus on the meetings, Belinda opened her computer and refined her notes. She added details to the quick items she'd written during the meetings. Working methodically, she ignored the called goodnights and dings of the elevator arriving and carrying people away. Her personal life sucked. She might as well focus on her new position. She was so much better at that than being a Little girl.

By eight, she'd exhausted the details in her memory. Belinda carefully saved the file and closed down her computer. Standing up on the tall pumps she'd covered the campus in today walking as she moved from meeting to meeting, Belinda promised herself she could wear flats tomorrow.

They'd contacted Sharon at lunch to give her the okay to continue the combined meetings. Each conversation with the department heads had gone swimmingly with both Pedro and her, gathering information that they would not have heard without the joint focus. There was no way Belinda could legitimately ask for Pedro to be scheduled separately.

Another day of waiting to see Pedro's disappointment with me or his anger at my rush for judgment against him, Belinda thought as she walked across the green space between Towers C and B.

Maybe it's time for me to move off campus.

That thought made her look around sadly. It was so pretty here. She hated to lose all this and the convenience of being close to work. Waving to the security guard on duty at the desk in Tower B, she headed upstairs to her apartment. Tinkerbell meowed loudly from outside her balcony door as she walked in.

The sight of the beautiful cat made her smile genuinely for the first time that day. Opening the door, she asked, "What are you doing here? You should be at home."

Tinkerbell sauntered in and elongated himself in a full body stretch before flopping over to show his belly. "Meow!"

"Are you lonely? Pedro must still be at the gym." She talked to the now purring creature as she sat down on the floor to pet Tink's tummy. "I really screwed up today, kitty. I ruined everything. I was a total bitch."

"Language, Little girl." Pedro stood in the balcony doorway. He wore shorts and a T-shirt. His hair was wet, cluing her in that he'd had time to work out and shower.

"Knox didn't kill you," she commented.

"He tried. That man is too tough for his own good." Pedro laughed before asking, "Can I come in?"

"I don't know why you want to," Belinda answered, keeping her head down as she stroked the cat in an attempt to keep him from seeing her cry.

Pedro accepted that as an invitation and settled next to her on the floor. He waited quietly for her to talk. When a sob escaped her lips, he lifted her easily onto his lap and rocked her slowly.

"Little girl. You are so hard on yourself."

"I ruined everything," she sobbed.

"What did you ruin?" he asked, smoothing back the hair from her face as she hid against his chest.

"Everything. I accused you of taking over my meetings and trying to sabotage me. None of it was your fault, and you were wonderful all day long."

"We figured it out. Misunderstandings happen, Little girl."

"You can't still want me to be that!" she wailed.

"My Little girl? Of course, you're mine. I have not searched for you for years, only to allow you to get scared and run away," he told her.

"I didn't run away. I was just… bitchy."

"Language. If I hear you call yourself a name again…"

She interrupted him, "You'll do what? Spank me again?" Sobs poured from her throat.

"If that's what you need to forgive yourself," Pedro reassured her gently. "Your first reaction was perfectly understandable. I would have bristled exactly like you did, Belinda."

"Bristled? That's a kind word for accusing you of trying to sabotage my new job after we just talked about it last night," she sobbed.

"The world is changing but technology has been a male-dominated field. I'm sure you've had a few roadblocks in your career."

When she nodded, he continued, "I would never expect you to

lower all your boundaries immediately. I think we made huge steps last night. Then today, all those past struggles crashed over your head, and it was easier to cling to those than take a risk with me."

Staring at him, Belinda whispered, "That's what happened. I felt like I was being torn in half. I wanted to believe you but kept remembering all the other people I hadn't been able to trust."

He was quiet for a few minutes as he rocked her. "Earning your trust is my first priority, Belinda. Have I done anything to make you think that you can't depend on me?"

"No," she admitted, sniffling.

"I think some type of punishment is exactly what you need, Little girl. It will wipe away all those negative thoughts and feelings and let you start fresh again. But this time, you'll have to decide to trust me. That means promising to talk to me in the future before jumping to a negative conclusion."

"I don't want another spanking," she wailed.

"I agree. The spanking relieved the tension you felt but didn't erase the thoughts lingering in your mind. Go get me some paper and a pen and take a seat at the table," he directed.

* * *

WHEN SHE WAS IN POSITION, he joined her. Several blank pages of computer paper and two pens sat in front of her. He loved that she was taking this seriously.

"What did you do wrong today, Little girl?" Pedro asked after taking a seat.

"Everything," she blurted.

"That isn't correct," he pointed out, refusing to let her take the easy way out. "Do you think you spoke kindly to your Daddy?"

"No," she admitted.

"Do you think you jumped to conclusions that were not correct without talking to me first?" he prompted.

She nodded her head.

"Use your words. I want to hear you say it."

"Yes," she whispered.

"Did you think the worst of me with nothing to lead you to suspect I was a bad person?"

"Yes."

"Are you afraid I won't want to be your Daddy anymore?"

"Who would want me? I screwed everything up." She looked at him desperately.

"I want you. I want the Little girl who struggles to trust her Daddy when he appears at the most unexpected time. I want the professional expert who has worked her way into an incredible leadership role and still seeks more. I want the woman who doesn't know that it's okay to live her truth—even if that truth conflicts with everything she's hidden behind. I know you're strong enough to accept all I want to give you and trust that I need you as much as you need me." Pedro waited a few seconds for his words to sink in.

"You do?" Belinda didn't allow herself to look back at him.

"I do. Now, for the misdeed of speaking ferociously to me without proof that I had done something underhanded, I want you to write, *Daddy only wants the best for me* twenty times."

Immediately, she bent to her task. He knew she needed to have something to focus on as she absorbed those words. She numbered them as she wrote, charming him with her efficiency.

"Done," she reported, putting her pen down with a click.

"Read them to me."

"All twenty of them?"

"Yes."

After a moment's hesitation, she followed his directions. One tear ran down her cheek as she finished. Pedro pulled his handkerchief from his pocket and leaned forward to wipe it away.

"That's true, isn't it?"

"Yes, Little one."

Without giving her time to think about that in more depth, he continued, "For jumping to conclusions before checking with me, write that line twenty more times."

"The same line?" she asked, looking at him in surprise.

"Does it apply?" he probed.

"Yes."

Taking a fresh sheet of paper, she copied the line again and again. He noticed that her precise lettering was becoming sloppier as her hand tired. She wrote without pausing as the words became integrated in her mind. A few more tears appeared on her cheeks and dropped to the paper below.

As she finished the last line, he instructed, "For thinking the worst of me, I'll cut this in half for ten sentences. In time, you will know for sure that I would climb mountains and fight rabid tigers for you, Little girl."

Sobs escaped from her lips as she scribbled those lines on the next sheet of paper.

"And finally, for being afraid that your Daddy would run away after one crappy life event happened, I'm going to hold you so close until you understand this Daddy is committed to you."

"What?" She looked up at him in surprise as he stood to tug the pen from her hand and drop it to the table before scooping her from the hard wooden chair. Taking her place, Pedro sat down to cuddle her in his lap. Taking her hand, he massaged her fingers until she relaxed against him.

"Good girl. Are you going to forget what you wrote tonight?" Pedro asked as he wiped her tears away.

"Never," she promised. "Do you forgive me?"

"Of course. But that punishment wasn't for me. It was to give you something to remember to say to yourself if questions pop up in your mind."

"Daddy only wants the best for me?" she repeated as if it were etched in her mind.

"Exactly."

Squeezing her tight, he rocked her gently. Tinkerbell climbed onto Belinda's lap and flopped down for pets. The trio sat together for several minutes as Belinda stroked the soft fur.

"Are you hungry?" Pedro asked, breaking the silence with such a normal question. It underlined his assertion that all the negatives were gone.

Belinda smiled at him tentatively. "I'm starving."

"Me, too. Let's see what's in your fridge. Tinkerbell, off," he commanded. The delightful purring machine hopped off her lap and stretched before moving out to the balcony.

"Come sit on a stool and talk to me." Pedro directed, picking up the pages she'd written on as they moved to the breakfast bar that separated the kitchen from the dining area. He helped her settle on a stool before attaching the pages in his hand to the refrigerator door with the magnets that decorated it.

He made himself at home, opening it and poking around at the contents inside. "I'll make us make-believe chicken quesadillas."

"I have that in my refrigerator?" she asked him in surprise.

"Almost."

She watched him chop leftover chicken as a pan heated. Using bread instead of tortillas, he grilled the treat on each side until golden brown. Pedro didn't allow Belinda to help. This was Daddy's job. She sipped the water he placed in front of her and munched on a few grapes he'd found when he searched her fridge.

As Pedro joined her at the counter, she realized she felt better than she had all day.

Leaning forward, she offered her lips to Pedro. He wrapped long fingers around the back of her head and held her close as he kissed her deeply. When he lifted his mouth from hers, his brown eyes were dark with need.

"Are you going to make love to me tonight?" she brazenly asked. He had no idea how much she was putting herself out there to even ask that.

"Not tonight. Tomorrow, if you are good," he promised.

"Another punishment?" she asked before she could stop herself.

"A reward. It's almost your bedtime. You've had a tough day. We'll celebrate our deepening relationship tomorrow."

She nodded. That made perfect sense, and it gave her more time to explain… stuff. Hiding a yawn, she picked up her fancy grilled sand-wich and took a bite. His arm wrapped around her for support and squeezed her tight.

CHAPTER 8

Purrs and soft kitty paw bops on her nose woke Belinda the next morning. She kissed Tinkerbell on the nose before stretching. The cat had chosen to stay with her last night again when Pedro had left her with instructions to lock the door behind him before showering and going to bed. He'd left the same way he'd come in earlier—vaulting from one balcony to the other.

Tinkerbell had vanished when she'd opened the balcony for him upon waking. This morning, her dynamic coworker had not been waiting outside for her. Leaving the door open as she got ready, Belinda hoped he would come visit and was understandably disappointed when Pedro had not made an appearance.

She let herself out the front door with her large travel cup of coffee when it was time to head to her office. "Oh!"

"Morning, Little girl." Pedro leaned in to kiss her, wrapping one arm around her waist to pull her close. He had been waiting outside her door for her to come out.

When he lifted his head, he said, "I've been looking forward to that since I woke up."

"You could have... You know, come in. I left the sliding glass door open for you."

"Then neither one of us would be at work on time."

He stepped back to scan her body, leaving no doubt in her mind that he appreciated the view. A thrill buzzed through her. She enjoyed seeing the desire on his face.

When he saw the coffee cup, Pedro asked, "Did you have breakfast?"

She lifted the cup to indicate the caffeinated beverage serving as her morning meal.

"That's not going to happen," he answered. Releasing her waist, he plucked the travel mug from her hand and replaced it with something very similar. This one had a straw. "Drink this first."

"Pedro, you don't want to mess with my coffee," she warned, looking at the other glass with disdain.

"Coffee is bad for you. Try the smoothie I made you."

"I don't really want to drink my food," she admitted.

He waggled her coffee cup and said nothing.

"That's not really food. Coffee is supposed to be a beverage. A smoothie is all blended up like you're too lazy to chew," Belinda pointed out.

"Or too busy." Pedro guided her down the hallway with a hand against her lower back.

Belinda eyed the smoothie suspiciously. "What did you put in it?"

"Good stuff that you'll love."

"Like spinach or kale? Everyone always tells me I'll enjoy them, but they just taste like what's left when the weed whacker goes too fast," Belinda smirked.

"Hmm. Guess you'll have to try it to find out."

They stepped into the elevator, and Pedro selected the ground floor. Belinda tried to read his expression to know whether he'd try to prank her with something awful or not.

"I'm never going to lie to you, baby," he whispered when they reached the bottom floor.

"All people lie," she answered.

"I'll keep in mind that you think so," he murmured as they stepped out into the bustling lobby. People headed in all directions to start their workday.

Belinda called her greetings in response to the hails of several people as they crossed the green space to their office building. Her mind shifted into work mode as she visualized her schedule she'd looked at earlier. Distracted, she lifted the cup to her lips and sucked on the straw.

"Wow! That's good. Does it have strawberries in it?" she asked.

"It does and I'm glad you like it," Pedro commented with a knowing glance.

"Okay. I should just listen to you," she admitted before whispering, "Daddy only wants the best for me."

"That will happen someday. For now, I need to prove to you I'm trustworthy. Just don't forget to put this as a win in my good Daddy column," he whispered to her.

Belinda nodded. He was always so nice when she automatically expected the worst from him. She needed to stop that. "Sorry."

"We'll talk about the men you've dated sometime. Remember, I'm different. Now, go do what the chief of technology does, and I'll go through all my email. I'll meet you at the elevator for our first meeting in forty-five minutes." With a wave, he wandered down the hallway toward his office.

It wasn't until she saw him take a drink from her coffee mug that she realized he'd never given it back. She looked down at the half-finished smoothie and lifted it to her lips. Drawing on the straw, she enjoyed the concoction and the view of his perfectly toned ass walking down the hall. *Mmm!*

* * *

"Okay, only one more day of meetings and you'll have met the leaders of the largest departments here on this Edgewater campus. There are others internationally, of course. My plan was to meet with them virtually next week," Belinda shared.

"Has your admin already booked those?" Pedro asked, glancing at her as they strolled back to Tower B at the end of the day.

"She has. Would you like to be included? Fair warning—she set some up in the middle of the night."

"Thank you for the invitation. I would like to join you. This is going well, I think. I've learned a lot that I think I wouldn't have immediately on my own. Everyone trusts and respects you. You've obviously built a reputation for being approachable and willing to help. I can tell why Easton chose you for your job."

"Thanks." She stared at him silently for a few seconds before admitting, "I really wanted to hate you even though I knew you were exactly what Edgewater Industries needed."

"I know," he said quietly. "In the world of consulting, you work with people for a short period. My job has been to jump in and make sweeping changes for a corporation. That always affects people's jobs. I stand behind everything I implement. Those were the necessary decisions, but I'm glad to be here for the long-term to alter the most important needs immediately and the lesser ones over time."

"Easton takes care of his people. He would have never hired a hatchet man," Belinda told him.

After nodding his agreement, Pedro asked, "Do you have time for dinner tonight?"

"Aren't you getting tired of me? We've spent a lot of time together."

"Never. I'd like to go for a run when I get home to unwind, then I'll come get you for dinner if you don't mind waiting."

"I don't mind." Belinda paused for a minute. "Could I run with you for a while? I'm not very athletic, but I've been sitting forever. I'd like to move a bit, too."

"I'd love it. It's a date."

She opened her mouth to comment on his choice of that word, but muffled sobs caught her attention. Searching for the source of the anguish, Belinda spotted Cynthia sitting on a bench. Her body language screamed that something was wrong.

"I have to go talk to her. Give me thirty minutes to see if I can help and change clothes?" Belinda asked Pedro.

"Of course. I don't want to leave you, but I don't know..." Pedro paused as he searched for her name.

"Cynthia. It's probably something work or man related. I'll pull in someone to help if I can't," Belinda promised with a small wave.

Heading for the culinary wizard in the Edgewater complex's cafeteria, Belinda wondered what could be happening. It looked like Cynthia's world had just exploded.

"Cynthia?" Belinda asked, sitting on the bench next to her. "Is everything okay?"

"No. It very definitely isn't okay," Cynthia almost laughed as she spit out that last word.

"What can I do?" Belinda asked.

"I don't think there's anything anyone can do." Cynthia looked at Belinda with wild eyes. "No one will believe me."

"I'll believe you, Cynthia," Belinda said firmly. She didn't know what was going on but was confident that the hardworking woman wasn't capable of anything serious.

"What's going on?" Belinda probed.

"He did it. He maneuvered and lied until everything was wrapped up in a neat packet. Please. I have to figure a way out of this. If something happens, would you talk to Mr. Edgewater and tell him I didn't do it vindictively? I wouldn't ever do this on my own," Cynthia pleaded.

"You're scaring me, Cynthia. Let's go talk to Easton together. He'll listen to whatever you need to tell him and... he'll help," Belinda urged. She stood and held out a hand to Cynthia. Easton would find time in his schedule if she escorted the woman to his office—even without her there, he'd talk to the visibly upset woman they all loved.

"It's too late. I've got to go." Cynthia stood and ran toward the parking lot. She pulled a set of keys from her pocket and jumped into a battered, older-model car. As Belinda watched, Cynthia drove toward the security gate.

What is going on?

Belinda shook her head. She headed back to Tower B to change.

Knox was behind the guard desk this afternoon. Belinda headed for the elevator and then changed course.

"Knox. I don't know what's going on, but I think someone should know."

"Definitely," he agreed.

Nodding her head at his agreement with her, Belinda shared, "I heard Cynthia crying."

"Cynthia Grant from the cafeteria?" he interrupted, grabbing his phone and making notes.

"Yes. She was looking at her phone like she'd gotten the worst news of her life. When I asked her if I could help, she asked me to tell Easton that she hadn't done it maliciously. Cynthia mentioned something about a man. He'd lied and maneuvered to wrap everything up in a neat package. She was really upset."

"That's not like Cynthia. Where is she now?"

"I tried to get her to go with me to talk to Easton, but she ran to her car and drove away."

Knox's eyebrows drew together as he paused in his notes. "She left?"

"Just a few minutes ago. I'll admit that I'm rattled by this. I don't know anything more about Cynthia other than she's the talented chef of amazing soups. Over the last year, I've spoken to her a dozen times. But I could feel the fright emanating from her. She was terrified."

Knox shook his head. The Daddy who had waited for his Little to be ready for him for years was on alert. "Thank you for telling me. I'll see if I can find her and get this settled."

"Thanks, Knox."

As the oversized security director plunged into investigation mode, Belinda walked across the lobby to the elevators. When a car opened, she stepped in and slumped against the metal wall. Talking to Cynthia had rattled her nerves. Arriving at her floor, she passed her apartment to reach Pedro's. She needed him.

"Hey!" Pedro's warm welcome shifted to concern as he scanned her face. Immediately, he pulled her close and wrapped his arms around her. Tinkerbell wove around her ankles, providing his support as well.

Belinda rested her face on his chest. *Thank goodness I found him.* The steady beat of his heart reassured her. After several long seconds, she raised her head to meet his gaze.

"Something's wrong. She wouldn't tell me any details. Cynthia's gone now. I stopped and told Knox. He's going to research whatever is happening."

"I'm glad you talked to him. Is there anything you need to do now?" he asked.

"There's nothing I can do but think of her."

"Send strength to her. She'll need that for whatever she's running from. Let's go run ourselves and burn off some of that negativity," Pedro suggested.

Nodding, Belinda said, "I'll go get changed. Give me five minutes."

"Hold on. I'll come with you. In, Tinkerbell," Pedro directed and shut the door after the cat wandered back into the apartment.

He took her hand and squeezed it gently. When they reached her door, Pedro followed her inside. She expected him to wait in the living room area. When he entered her bedroom, Belinda said quickly, "I'll be just a minute."

"Daddy's going to help you, baby."

"Get dressed?" she whispered. She'd been over his lap half naked. Why did this seem so intimate?

"Find a pair of shoes, shorts, a sports bra, and a T-shirt," he directed from the center of the room.

Belinda scrambled to find all the items she needed. Passing him several times on her path, she checked his expression to see if he'd become exasperated with all her delays to their run. His face remained composed and pleasant.

"I'm sorry I'm slowing you down," she blurted when she passed him the next time.

Pedro stepped in front of her and ran his hands down her arms. "Are you nervous about me seeing your beautiful body?" When she hesitated, he stroked over her bottom and squeezed one cheek.

She took a deep breath and told the truth. Lying to him wasn't an option. "Yes."

"You will be nothing less than perfect in my eyes." When she opened her mouth to speak, he continued, "No matter what you've decided you don't like about your body, I can assure you that I won't see any flaws. You are my Little. The one I've looked to find for what seems like forever. Even if you had a penis and an extra head, I would treasure you."

"A penis?" She had to laugh. "I don't have one of those."

"I know." He waggled his eyebrows suggestively and she remembered with a flood of heated embarrassment that he had probably seen everything during her spanking.

"Okay," she whispered.

"Good girl. Let's get this pretty blouse off."

His fingers nimbly unfastened the buttons, flicking across her breasts and abdomen in casual contact that felt like mini lightning bolts. The white fabric gaped open as he reached the last fastener. With that open, he slid the silky material over her shoulders and allowed it to tumble to the floor at her feet.

Belinda dropped her eyes to the front of his T-shirt to avoid his gaze. A slow motion caught her eye as Pedro's hand shifted across the front of his short jogging shorts to adjust his hardening shaft before unzipping the side zipper of her tailored skirt and letting it glide downward. She couldn't control the smile that curled her lips as she studied his lengthening reaction to her body.

"I may have to put ice down my pants before we start," Pedro leaned in to whisper against her ear.

A happy giggle tumbled from her lips. "Sorry?"

"You're not sorry at all. Careful, we know what happens when you lie to Daddy," he reminded her with a firm pat to her still sore bottom.

"I'm being good," she reminded him.

He knelt at her feet to unfasten her sensible sandals. "Step," he instructed as he removed each shoe and the fabric looped around her feet.

When she was free, he rose effortlessly to reach around her

ribcage. His fingertips caressed the lace that decorated the edge. The ease with which he unfastened the bra sent a shiver of anger through her. How many of these had he removed? She didn't want to think of him with other women.

Sliding the straps from her shoulders, he drew the lacy garment from her body. Pedro flicked the bra away and cupped her breasts. His fingers traced her curves and brushed over her tight nipples, drawing a groan from her mouth. Belinda bit her bottom lip, trying to stay quiet.

"Don't hide anything from Daddy, Little girl. Let me hear your sweet sounds," he corrected sternly, lifting one hand from her breast to smooth over her trapped lip.

She nodded and exhaled quietly as he stepped away to grab her sports bra. Wrangling the supportive garment into place had them both laughing by the end. Belinda loved how he reached inside to adjust each breast's position within the cups to make sure she was comfortable.

In minutes, he'd finished dressing her. Bouncing on her sneakers, Belinda was eager to go. Pedro captured her attention as he adjusted his heavy shaft inside his shorts. She quickly looked away as heat flushed her cheeks, but inside, she loved how much he responded to taking care of her.

"I'll get myself under control, Belinda. You'll just have a new job of walking in front of me as we head outside into the fresh air," Pedro teased, intercepting her furtive glance. "Can you do that for me, Little girl?"

"Yes, D..."

"It's okay to call me Daddy, Belinda."

"I know. It just seems like a big step. Daddy, in my mind, comes with so much emotion, control, submission... Especially after I screwed things up, trying to use it like a joke. Now, it's like saying I love you. I don't fling that around either. I want it to be special."

Pedro pulled her to him and hugged her tight against his hard frame. "You'll know when it's the right time for you to say it. Let's go run. This afternoon has been filled with dra-ma!" He emphasized the two syllables of the last word, making her laugh.

"I'm ready."

Preceding him down the hallway, Belinda looked over her shoulder when Pedro groaned. His gaze was focused on her bottom.

"Want me to walk behind you now?" she teased.

"Then I'd feel you watching my ass," he teased her back, taking her hand and pulling her into the elevator. "I don't think that would help either. Tell me about the safeguards you install on computers before assigning them to employees."

"Distract you with techy stuff, huh?"

"That might not even help but try it."

They dropped the conversation when they emerged from the tower and launched into a slow run together. Belinda knew that he was holding back as they made a big loop around the grounds. When he didn't seem unhappy to modify his pace to allow her to join him, she chose not to worry about it.

Eventually, she knew it was wise for her to stop before making herself too sore to walk the next day. "I'm going to walk down this path and take a seat on one of the benches outside Tower B to enjoy the fresh air. Take your time finishing your run."

"You did well. I'll make a few laps and we'll go have dinner."

She slowed to a walk and watched him speed up to a much quicker pace. Belinda knew he'd push himself to maximize his workout. That was the type of person Pedro was. He didn't tackle life by half measures. He committed himself fully to everything he did. *Including being a Daddy.*

CHAPTER 9

"Eat three more bites," Pedro instructed as they sat at the table together.

"I really don't like spinach," she admitted, poking at the leafy salad he'd made to go along with the omelet he'd whipped up for their dinner.

"Then pick the carrots and celery out and crunch on those," he suggested.

"I can do that," she agreed happily. "Do you want my spinach?"

Pedro snaked an arm across the table to stab a few leaves. "Sure. Just call me Popeye," he joked with a wink.

"I don't think you need anything to make you stronger," she commented, eying his muscular arms revealed by the tank shirt he wore.

"Everyone needs nutrients to be strong." He stabbed a few more before asking, "Have you been tested lately?"

"Tested?" she echoed, not following his train of thought.

"For anything we could transmit to each other," he explained gently. "My plan is to clean the kitchen before cleaning us up. I don't think I can keep my hands off you in the shower, Little girl. Do I need to bring condoms?"

"Oh! That kind of testing."

Belinda felt her face heat with embarrassment. She was absolutely poised and confident in a work situation. In an intimate setting, Belinda felt like a fish out of water. Last night, she'd blurted an invitation for him to make love to her in a surge of desire-fueled bravery. How did she tell him that she'd had boyfriends before but hadn't ever chosen to have sex with any of them? He was going to think that her choices were wacky.

"I've had all the standard communicable disease screenings that apply for me," she answered cagily.

"There are some that aren't suitable for you?" he asked with a look of confusion.

"I'm a virgin," she blurted before she could stop herself. "I know that's completely weird, and you may wish to run the other way."

Pedro set his fork down with a clink and stood. Rounding the table, he picked her up and sat down in her chair with Belinda on his lap. "I'm not running anywhere for any reason. Especially not because you've chosen to wait for someone you think is special before taking this step."

"I'm most likely the only virgin on the entire Edgewater campus and you got stuck with her."

"I am not stuck with you. I chose you. Am I surprised? Yes. Am I repelled? Hell, no."

Belinda had already observed that Pedro wasn't against swearing when the situation merited it outside of a workplace situation, but he seemed to only curse to underline something important. "Really?"

"To know that my Little girl feels having sex as something so private, it's not a part of her she wants to share with others is definitely okay. Had you chosen to be with a hundred men, that could have been okay too, as long as the relationships with other men happened before ours. I'm not okay with cheating."

"Oh! Me, neither. How could you do that? If you don't love someone with all your heart, it's better to not be intimate with them." Her mouth snapped shut as she realized what she'd revealed.

"You've never been in love, Belinda?" he probed.

"No. I thought I was, but I must not have been because it was never enough. I'd decided recently that I was being ridiculous and needed to just go for it. That's why I asked you to make love to me before. Why keep waiting?"

"Because it's the right thing for you?" he suggested.

"Maybe? Or maybe, I just need to give up on childhood dreams of what relationships are supposed to be."

"Never give up on your dreams, Little girl. Thank you for telling me. We'll wait until you're ready and I'll know to protect you from pregnancy when we take that step."

"I think I'm ready with you," she blurted quickly.

"When you're ready, you'll know. You won't have to think." Pedro kissed her softly. "You are the treasure of my life. While I want to sink deep inside you until we don't know where you stop and I begin, I don't mind waiting. You are totally worth it."

"I'm sorry…"

"Don't be sorry for telling me how you truly feel. I'm grateful you trust me."

She nodded. He understood. How did he always know the right thing to say?

"Okay, dishes first and then into the shower because it will be time for bed soon."

"I wish we could take a shower together."

"Oh, I plan on giving you a shower."

"You're funny," she laughed, relaxing against his hard body for the first time since he'd picked her up to have the intimate conversation.

When he didn't laugh with her, Belinda snuck a glance at him. Pedro kissed her before correcting her, "This Daddy doesn't joke about taking care of his baby girl."

"I'm not a baby," she protested.

"Maybe not all the time," he agreed. "Up. Let Daddy clean up the dishes."

"I can help," she volunteered.

"Daddy's job. You sit at the counter and talk to me."

When he was back in the kitchen and she was perched on a stool with Tinkerbell on her lap, Pedro observed, "You've stolen my cat's affection."

"No! He still loves you best. I just give good scratches." Belinda demonstrated, finding a perfect spot under the cat's jawline.

"Have you ever had animals?" he asked.

"I grew up out in the country. We had an assortment of animals thanks to people who drop their animals off in the middle of nowhere."

Pedro shook his head slowly. "Those people are going to have a fiery place waiting for them at the end of their lives. Tink wouldn't be alive if I hadn't spotted him. I bet the same fate would have befallen on those lucky animals that found refuge with your family."

Belinda nodded before pointing out, "Tinkerbell looks pretty happy now."

"He definitely learned quickly that I had love and a happy home to share. Even if he does have to ride around in my car every once in a while."

"Only one more time—when you move to a house."

"I won't leave you here. When a house is ready, and when you're ready to move with me, I'll check out a larger place on the Edgewater campus somewhere," he told her as he put the last plate in the dishwasher.

"You want me to move in with you?"

"You're my Little girl. You belong with your Daddy."

The conviction in his words made her heart skip a beat. Each moment that she spent with Pedro helped her have confidence in their relationship. He just seemed to get her.

"Time for your shower. Sweaty clothes off," Pedro announced as he led her into the bathroom.

It was a modest size. Just perfect for one person to move around in. Add his large body and the space became much more intimate. Belinda shifted as Pedro turned on the water in the shower to warm.

"I miss having a tub," she told him, trying to make light conversation to disperse the sexual tension growing inside her.

"We'll build a house with a big tub and shower space for us. Little girls need bubble baths," Pedro said as he pulled her top over her head.

When her face popped free of the material, Belinda asked, "You take bubble baths?"

"I could be convinced to do just about anything to make my Little happy."

Belinda didn't know what to say to that. She stood still as Pedro pushed her shorts and panties to her ankles and knelt in front of her to remove her shoes and the rumpled clothing. When he stood, she only wore her sports bra.

Nervous, she crossed her hands in front of her pubic area to shield herself from his view. Belinda jumped when Pedro moved her hands to her sides.

"Don't hide from Daddy."

Belinda nodded like she understood. Inside, she forced herself to stand there as he raised his hands to remove her last garment. *He's seen you naked. Stop freaking out!*

"It's okay, Belinda. Lift your arms." He smoothly removed her bra and dropped it to the pile of clothes on the floor. Pedro's hands smoothed down her sides. "Go jump in the shower," he instructed with a smart pop to her bottom.

Immediately, she whirled to step through the door into the spray. His swat hadn't hurt, she realized, and was disappointed. She'd liked having a reminder of her spanking. It made her remember that he cared.

A rustle from outside the stall made her wipe the spray from the frosted glass. She leaned forward to see more clearly as he revealed more of his bronze skin as he stripped. When he dropped his shorts, she straightened away from the barrier and heard him chuckle.

"I'm coming in there with you, Little girl," he reminded her as he opened the door.

Deliberately, she kept her gaze on his face. "Hi! I'm almost done."

"Tip your head back into the water. I'll wash your hair first. That way the conditioner can soak in for a while."

Closing her eyes, she followed his directions. This seemed safe. He moved closer to run his fingers through her hair to make sure it was thoroughly wet, his hard body coming in contact with hers as he reached around her.

She inhaled sharply and held her breath until he stepped back and directed her to turn around. Exhaling, she obeyed. Belinda felt the shampoo land on her wet hair before his fingers returned to massage the lather through her thick hair. The water sprayed into her face as she enjoyed the feel of him rubbing over her scalp and the length of her blonde strands. Without thinking, she leaned back slightly to balance herself against his muscular frame.

"Oh!" she gasped and darted forward, only to feel his hand spread across her abdomen to pull her back against him. She tried not to squeeze her bum together as she felt his erection nestle between her buttocks.

"You're okay, Little girl. My body craves yours but I'm in control." He continued to wash her hair without pausing.

She peeked over her shoulder to see him wink at her. "Should I rinse my hair?" she suggested, trying to give herself a break from the arousing feel of him against her.

"Sure. Turn around."

This time when she faced Pedro, he wrapped an arm around her waist to allow her to lean back into the spray. This arched her lower body directly against his pelvis. She moaned in arousal.

"You feel good against me, too," he reassured her as he rinsed the suds out with one hand before having her turn around to allow him to apply conditioner to her wet hair. Quickly, he washed and rinsed the makeup from her face.

Pedro rinsed his hands before moving between her and the spray of water. He pumped her favorite body wash onto one hand and smoothed it over her shoulders and arms. When he dispensed more, she knew what he'd wash next. His fingers closed around her breasts, circling her curves and brushing over her nipples. The sight of his hands moving on her body made Belinda clench her thighs together as his touch pushed her arousal higher. When he stroked lower to spread the silky soap over her abdomen, Belinda stepped back in an attempt to calm herself.

"Come back, Little girl. Stand right there," Pedro directed with a firm voice as he pointed to the spot right in front of her.

"I can wash there," she told him quickly.

"Who's the Daddy?"

"You are?" she answered tentatively.

"I am. Daddy makes the rules. Come stand here."

When she inched her way back to where he indicated, Pedro kissed her lightly. "I know you're aroused. I am, too. That's the way it's supposed to be."

Belinda nodded. She'd never felt attracted to anyone this much. Pedro checked off every box on her wish list: handsome, intelligent, sexy, skilled, and oh, so Daddy. Wrapping her arms around Pedro's shoulders, Belinda closed her eyes when Pedro directed her to widen her legs. She felt his fingers glide through the curls guarding her most intimate area. He would know very soon just how turned on she was. There would be no secret of her response to him.

He traced the seam of her sex before pressing his palm against her to cup the area. "So hot," he praised. "Such a good girl."

His fingers dipped between her lower lips to trace her pink folds. Pedro circled her clit with one fingertip before brushing rapidly over the top of it. Belinda rose involuntarily to her tiptoes to encourage him to pleasure her more. Pedro's touch combined with his low chuckle of approval made her body flood with slick juices. She struggled not to respond. When his touch lifted from her body, she opened her eyes in shock.

"Let's get this soap rinsed off. I don't want anything to sting your delicate bits," he told her as he stepped to the side out of the spray to allow the water to pour onto her skin. Pedro smoothed one hand over her torso to help free her skin of suds as he stroked the other soapy one over her bottom.

"We can't forget to clean here," he whispered. When she started to bolt away, he held her secure against his body as his fingers dipped into the cleft between her buttocks.

Teasing the small opening hidden there, Pedro asked in a low tone, "Have you ever touched yourself here? Pressed a plug into place as you played?"

His words painted an erotic picture in her mind. With Pedro, nothing would be off limits. He would ask everything of her and make sure she enjoyed it. She shivered in reaction as she imagined something invading her body. He tightened his arm to secure her to his hard body and pressed one fingertip against that clenched opening, making her fantasies come true.

"Daddy?" she whispered, without realizing what she'd called him.

"Your Daddy's right here. I've got you," he reassured her in a low tone as that finger pushed just inside her entrance. The soap slightly burned that ring of muscles, reinforcing his mastery over her.

Her needy moan echoed against the hard surfaces of the shower. Belinda only realized that it had come from her throat when she heard the sound. Her wordless protest followed that sound as he removed his finger to turn her around to rinse the lather from her skin.

Looking at him, Belinda watched him clean his hands with a quick whisper that he needed to take care of her. She didn't understand what he meant until he lowered himself to kneel before her.

"Brace yourself on my shoulders, Little girl, and widen your legs." Those instructions registered somewhere in her pleasure-fogged mind.

When her fingers gripped the corded muscles of his body, Pedro told her, "Baby girl. Daddy wants to see you come on my fingers. Will you do that for me?"

Nodding instantly, Belinda felt his fingers stroke her pussy. This time, he pressed a finger deep into her as his thumb stroked over her clit. She knew he watched her body's reaction to his touch. His tongue tasted the top of her cleft, making her jump.

His whispered, "Shhh!" against her sent vibrations through her before he moved one hand to cup her bottom and draw her forward to his lips and caressing touch. Pedro circled her clit with his lips and sucked gently before pulling it strongly into his mouth.

With a scream of completion, Belinda exploded, feeling waves of pleasure rock her body as he held her steady against him. When she calmed, Pedro rose to his feet and held her close.

"That was pretty, Little girl. I'll need to see that a million more times. Stay here in the warm water," he directed, stepping away from her. He pumped a bit of soap onto his hands and spread the flowery scent over himself.

Belinda leaned against the glass enclosure, watching his hands move over his body. It was so hot. She'd seen naked men before but not wet, right in front of her, and touching themselves. She took a step toward him and froze when Pedro shook his head. Holding her gaze, he wrapped his soapy hand around his erection and pulled hard from root to tip.

"Little girls have to earn permission to touch their Daddies."

She stared at him. "Permission?"

"Yes, Little girl. You need to have my permission to touch yourself as well. I will take your vibrator from your drawer this evening when I leave."

"How did you know..." she began and then bit her lip. *He knows all my secrets.*

Pedro lifted his head in a purely masculine nod as if he could read her thoughts. His hand moved faster on his thick cock. Focused completely on the rough movements, Belinda was fascinated as he pushed himself toward a climax. Wishing she could be the one touching him, she tried to memorize what he enjoyed. She knew someday she'd be allowed to caress him.

"Touch yourself," he growled at her.

Belinda looked at him in confusion. Did he mean...? The fire in his eyes left no question in her mind. Amazed that she wasn't embarrassed, Belinda widened her legs and ran her fingertips through the slick juices that had escaped the water streaming against her back. She was so turned on. The world could have ended around them and Belinda wouldn't have noticed. There was only her Daddy and her.

"Ah!" she cried into the small space as her body contracted into the strongest orgasm she'd ever felt.

His shout rang out, blending with hers as she watched him explode. She took a step forward and froze. Belinda remembered she didn't have permission to touch her Daddy.

"Good girl," he praised her as his hand gentled on his shaft. In a few seconds, he walked forward into the stream of water to cup her face. His lips seized hers in a fierce kiss that she felt throughout her body. "I had begun to despair that I would never find you, Little girl. My search for you was worth every moment of loneliness."

The tender kiss that followed seemed to reach every cell in her body. Belinda wrapped one arm around his neck and clung to the man that had turned her world upside down. Pressing her hand to his chest, she felt his heartbeat under her palm.

"Thank you!" She mentally sent the message out into the world. She owed whoever or whatever had brought the two of them together. Thank goodness, she hadn't gotten his job.

Belinda let him rinse the lingering juices from her inner thighs and pussy. His touch sent vibrations through her body. She'd never responded to anyone like she did to Pedro.

Once they stepped out of the shower—picking a clear spot in the midst of all the scattered clothing—Pedro dried her carefully as if he understood her skin felt electrified by the shattering passion they had shared. After wrapping a towel around his waist, he brushed out her damp hair, brushed her teeth, and smoothed her favorite face cream into her skin.

"Do you have any medicine to take before bed?" he asked as he cared for her.

"No." Belinda yawned and glanced at the clock in amazement. "I can't go to bed now."

"Little girls need more sleep than others do. Do we need to dry your hair?"

"No, I always sleep on it wet," she answered with another yawn.

"Then let me tuck you into bed before you fall asleep on your feet."

He led her into her bedroom and turned down the covers. Locating her sleepshirt under her pillow, he dropped it over her head.

"Under the covers, baby girl," he directed, holding the sheet up for her to slide inside.

He tucked the sheets around her chin before looking around the room. She held her breath as he walked to her dresser and scooped the plush platypus up gently to carry it to her bed.

Her Daddy stroked the fur softly before asking, "What's his name?"

"Her name," Belinda corrected, "is Bubbles."

Pedro turned the creature around to speak to her personally. "I am glad to meet you, Bubbles. Keep my Little safe, please."

He held her up to his ear and listened before answering, "Thank you, Bubbles."

Gently, he tucked her into Belinda's arms and kissed her temple. Through heavy eyelids, she watched him open her nightstand and remove the lubricant and the small wand vibrator. "Daddy will hold on to this for you. Sleep, baby girl."

Belinda closed her eyes. She heard him moving around her apartment for a few minutes. She was so tired and quickly lost her battle to stay awake.

CHAPTER 10

Belinda was almost sad to end the last of her meetings with the department heads. She and Pedro had worked together to gather a lot of information that they could both profit from in the future.

As they walked back to Tower B at the end of the day, Belinda confessed, "I'm going to miss seeing you in all my meetings."

Pedro wrapped an arm around her waist and hugged her to his side. "I'll miss seeing you all day as well, but I have a feeling we'll run into each other a lot. Would you like to schedule lunch together unless we have some sort of meeting or emergency?"

"Let's. And we'll see each other after work," she pointed out.

"Of course. What would you like to do tonight?" he asked. "Do you like biking?"

"I haven't ridden a bike since the fifth grade," she said with a laugh.

"Your muscle memory would take over," he assured her.

"Probably. Pedro, I know from your bio that triathlons are important to you. I don't want to get in the way of your training," she hedged, not wanting him to think she would try to keep him with her every moment of the day. Belinda was sure clingy women were the bane of men's existence.

"Thank you for caring about me. Physical activity is important to me. It's how I deal with stress. At times, my job will be hard core. I'll need to burn off the adrenaline."

"I can understand that. Coordinating all these departments is going to push me more than I've ever been before, too," Belinda confessed. "I go to a yoga class with Fane—he's Elaine's administrative assistant. He picked out your admin, remember?"

"Of course. He found someone perfect for me. Elaine... Rivers, right? She's Easton's second-in-command?" Pedro asked, trying to put all the pieces together.

"I bet your brain is ready to explode with all these names."

"There are a lot of new faces to remember, that's for sure. I'll get them all sorted soon. In the meantime, I cheat and look over the website to match people and pictures."

"That's a great idea. I might do that myself when I run into people I don't quite have memorized," Belinda laughed.

They arrived at Tower B and walked into the large lobby. Just walking through the door separated them. Belinda missed his arm around her. A movement caught her attention, and she pointed to the security desk.

Knox waved. When Pedro looked his way, Knox called, "I'm working out tonight if you're up for leg night."

Without thinking, Belinda looked down at Pedro's legs. *Nice. They're even better when he doesn't wear pants.* Realizing she was checking him out in public, Belinda yanked her gaze back to Knox's face. She knew he suspected they were more than neighbors by the gigantic man's smile.

"Maybe? I'll see what I feel like when I get my clothes changed. When are you starting?" Pedro asked.

"Twenty minutes," Knox supplied.

With a wave, they walked to the elevator and entered with several friends. The Friday afternoon camaraderie was strong as everyone celebrated the weekend. Even working for an incredible company like Edgewater Industries, everyone looked forward to two free days to enjoy.

When the car stopped at their floor, Pedro and Belinda were the only ones to exit. Belinda loved that the handsome man walking next to her instantly rested his hand at her waist.

"You should go for it. You know… Exercise with Knox. I can relax and do my nails."

"I could be an expert manicurist," Pedro offered.

"A Daddy that knows his way around fingernail polish?"

"Find me a video. I can do it. I have some of my mom's tamales frozen in my freezer. I can zap those and fix a salad after working out. Then we can do your nails."

"Do you really want to do that? I can do it myself," she assured him.

"Your job is to curl up with Bubbles to watch some girly program and relax as you search the internet for a relatively easy way for me to decorate your nails. You'll need to choose colors, of course, too."

It sounded like fun to have him try to do her nails. Belinda could always take it off if he did a lousy job. There really wasn't a risk. Besides, she was exhausted after all the meetings this week. Being a technology person meant you usually worked alone with a pile of data or coding to keep you company. She genuinely liked people, but this week had been people overload.

"I like tamales," she agreed with a smile as they reached her door.

"Want to hang out at my place?"

"You want me to watch TV in your apartment?"

"Yes. Let's get your clothes changed and grab Bubbles. You can keep Tinkerbell company and… I like the thought of you in my home. It will give me energy to whomp Knox's butt for leg night."

"I've seen Knox's butt. I don't think I'd plan on kicking it if I were you," she warned as they walked into her apartment and headed for her bedroom.

"One, no looking at Knox's butt. Two, my butt will never be that large. He's like a giant." His dancing dark eyes told her he was teasing.

Giggling at his sense of humor, Belinda qualified her acceptance. "I'll come if you have snacks."

"Cheese popcorn?" he suggested.

"The white cheddar kind or the orange kind?"

"White cheddar, of course."

"Then I accept."

Belinda tried not to get nervous as Pedro followed her into her bedroom. He'd already seen and touched virtually every part of her. Still, as he undressed her, she had to keep herself from shielding her body from his gaze. She tried to focus on the small things he did to make her more comfortable—rubbing her feet after removing her shoes, insisting she didn't need a bra, and helping her into slouchy sweatpants and a baggy T-shirt.

"I don't look very good for a date," she pointed out, waving a hand at her outfit.

"Are you ready to relax?" he probed.

"Definitely."

"Then it's time to head to my apartment. Grab Bubbles and let's take your polish with us."

"You're really going to do my nails?" she asked.

"Yes. Why not? It sounds like fun to me."

She couldn't prevent the delighted giggle that burst from her lips. Belinda picked up her stuffie from the bed, grabbed her phone to look for videos, and darted into the bathroom to pull the small basket of nail polish from the storage closet. Reporting back to Pedro, she almost danced in excitement before him.

"I'm ready."

"You need shoes to be out in the hall."

"Nope. I'm not wearing shoes," she declared.

"Give me the basket," he requested. When she complied, he leaned over and scooped her up over one shoulder in a fireman's lift.

Squealing, she grabbed the back of his pants for security. "I can walk!"

"Not without shoes. Let's go." Pedro walked with no apparent difficulty to the door and out into the hall. He held on to her with one hand while the other held the basket of polish.

"Daddy!" she whispered furiously as he paused at his door to open it. "People are coming. Put me down."

"Hold this," Pedro requested, swinging his arm behind him to hand her the basket.

Belinda grabbed it as the voices approached the turn in the hall. She sighed in relief as he stepped inside and closed the door behind him. "That was close!"

Pedro set her feet down on the carpet and pulled her close. Brushing the hair from her face, he asked, "Would it be that bad if people knew we were involved?"

Studying his concerned face, she shook her head and admitted, "No. I don't really care if they know. I've just always been cautious about separating my career and my private life."

"How about if I promise I'll never discuss our intimate activities with anyone?"

"I'll make the same promise," she answered eagerly.

With that settled, Belinda looked around the room, comparing her space to Pedro's.

"Then we're set. Do you want to talk to Daddy as I change or just flop on the couch and relax?"

Feeling her eyes widen at the thought of watching him strip down, Belinda nodded without trusting herself to answer with words. His answering low chuckle told her he'd followed her thought pattern.

"Come on, Little girl." Pedro took her hand and led her to the bedroom.

"Hop up on the bed," he instructed and wrapped his hands around her waist. As she jumped, he lifted her to sit on the mattress before shrugging out of his jacket and tugging his tie free.

"Better!" he said in relief.

She watched his fingers nimbly unbutton his white dress shirt. His tanned chest appeared as the fabric gaped open. Belinda squirmed on the comforter, feeling herself become wet. She bit her lip when he unfastened his belt and pants to pull his shirttails out.

"What big eyes you have, Little girl."

Her gaze shot to his face and she knew she looked guilty. "Sorry."

"You don't need to apologize. I like that you are attracted to me."

"Attracted?" she echoed. *Oh, this is way past attracted...*

His chuckle made her realize that she'd said that aloud instead of in her head. Belinda slapped one hand over her mouth. The other hand covered the first when she moaned as he pushed his slacks to the floor.

"Knox is going to think I like him way too much if I show up in this condition, Little girl," Pedro commented before waving a hand over his thickening shaft now pressing against the cotton material of his snug boxer briefs.

Taking this for an invitation, Belinda slid off the bed and cupped her Daddy's erection.

"Do you have permission to touch your Daddy?" he asked sharply. Pedro loved that his Little girl had acted without thinking. Her body drew him instinctually as well.

"N-No," she mumbled.

He stepped out of his shoes and clothing, dislodging her hands, which had not moved. "Time for you to go cool off in the corner for sixty seconds." Turning Belinda around so she faced away from him, Pedro sent her jumping forward with a stinging swat to her curvy bottom.

* * *

"Ouch!" Looking over her shoulder, Belinda stumbled forward to take her place in the corner. She felt uncomfortable there as she focused on the walls before her. The rustle behind her became too intriguing, and she turned her head to look.

"Eyes forward," he barked as her head rotated.

"Hrumpf!" She grumpily put her forehead against the paint.

"Hi, Tinkerbell," Belinda greeted the cat who appeared and curled around her legs to provide a distraction and keep her company. "I'm in corner jail." The purring creature meowed his sorries and disappeared behind her.

Left in the small space, Belinda listened to the rustle behind her. He'd be naked now. The temptation to see his chiseled body almost made her look, but she forced herself to stay where he'd sent her.

She'd always laughed at this punishment in books. *It's brutal. Worse than a spanking!*

Okay, not really, but it was like watching paint dry. So boring… And uncomfortable. Belinda amused herself by counting the ways a Daddy could punish a Little girl. She had just visualized an anal plug when Pedro's hand cupped one buttock.

"I'll give you a dollar if you'll tell me what you're thinking about so hard that this bottom is wiggling."

"What?" she gasped and turned around to meet his amused gaze. "I wasn't thinking about anything. I… I had an itch."

Pedro shook his head and tugged her out of the corner. "Little girls shouldn't lie to their Daddies. They always know. Come on, baby. I'm finished dressing. Let's get you relaxed on the couch."

"I didn't like standing in the corner."

"You were there for fifty-two seconds, baby girl. You really wouldn't like it if that had been a punishment."

"That wasn't a punishment?" she asked as she sat down in the living room.

"If you are fully dressed, you aren't being punished for anything. That was simply keeping you out of trouble, so you didn't wind up in the corner with at least your bottom on display," Pedro explained as he moved around the room.

"I'll be good," she promised.

"Thank you, Belinda."

Within a couple of minutes, Pedro had Belinda settled on the couch with water, a snack, Bubbles, her phone, and the remote. He kissed the top of her head before reminding her, "I'm a phone call away."

"Enjoy! I'll be right here. Don't hurry."

CHAPTER 11

Pedro let himself quietly into the apartment. Knox had helped him push hard during the workout. The immense man was well trained in techniques to build strength. Pedro had already made the commitment to join him regularly. More long lean muscle would help Pedro in future triathlons. Knox had even offered his private cove for swimming practice.

"Daddy?" Belinda called.

"I'm here. Did you find something to watch on TV?"

"I love this movie. I missed it in the theater."

"Awesome, baby girl. Keep watching. I'll shower and get food ready. I bet I'll get here in time to see the end with you and Bubbles."

She nodded before looking back at the screen. Her rapt expression reassured him she'd be okay for a few more minutes.

Quickly, he jumped into the shower. Standing under the cold water, he lathered the sweat away and dipped his head under the spray. Her greeting repeated in his mind. Belinda didn't realize that she called him Daddy automatically when caught off guard. He couldn't believe how much he cared for her already. She'd intrigued him in the online seminar. In person, she was sexy, adorable, intelligent, hardworking, and yes, just as he'd expected, one hundred percent Little girl.

"*My* Little girl," he corrected himself.

He quickly dressed in sweatpants and jogged to the kitchen. In a flash, Pedro had created a family-style dinner of an enormous bowl of salad, a plate filled with steaming tamales, and a tall glass of water for him. He carried the tray to the couch and pushed Tinkerbell gently off the cushion to make room for himself. Laughing at the cat's affronted glare, Pedro sat next to Belinda who sniffed the aroma eagerly and leaned against him.

Pedro wrapped an arm around her shoulders and cut a bite of tamale. Lifting it to her lips, he smiled as she took a bite and moaned her approval, chewing as the suspenseful music of the movie's climax wrapped around them. He took a bite and offered her another before pressing a kiss to her hair. It looked like his mother's secret recipe had another fan.

When the movie ended, Belinda turned off the TV. Turning back to Pedro, she shook her head at the bite he offered. "No more for me. Those are incredible. You said your mom made them. Think she'd teach me?"

The minute the words escaped from her mouth, Belinda's eyes widened as she processed how that might sound to Pedro. "I mean... Maybe, someday, if we have a chance to meet... she might show me or give me some tips?" With every carefully chosen word that emerged from her mouth, he could tell that she was kicking herself.

"You will meet *mi mamá*. She can't wait to meet you and will definitely teach you anything you would like to learn," Pedro told her with a smile. "Would you like to see a picture of my family?"

"Please."

Placing the tray on the table, he pulled out his phone and flipped through the pictures. "Here's one of all my immediate family." He handed her the snapshot of him on a family vacation two years ago.

"These are your parents and brothers and sisters? A cousin or two mixed in maybe?" she suggested, looking at the large group.

"Nope. Those are all my siblings." He pointed to each person and shared each one's name and age.

"How old are you?"

"I'm the oldest. I'm thirty-seven."

"You don't look that old," she said, waving away the bite of salad he offered her.

"Thanks, baby girl. And you're thirty-one. Are you okay being stuck with an old man?"

"You're not that old," she dismissed his suggestion. "How did you know how old I am?"

"I'm the king of internet searches. I could tell you what size bra you buy online," he joked.

"Did you look to see what my bra size is?" she asked, leaning away.

"No, Little girl. I won't invade your privacy. I will be transparent. If you are in danger, I will search through everything in the chance there is a clue to save you."

"You'd care that much to search for me?" she asked quietly.

"You are *mi corazón*, Little girl. My heart. I can't lose you."

A tear rolled from the corner of her eye and trailed down her cheek. When he wiped it away, she pressed her cheek into his hand. "I can't believe I feel this strongly about you. It's crazy. We just met."

"It's crazy wonderful. Time doesn't matter, Little girl. This is what matters." He pressed a hand to her heart. "What does your heart say?"

"That you're part of me."

"That's what mine says, too," he shared.

Pedro loved the smile that spread over her lips. He leaned in to kiss her lightly. "Now, *mi corazón*, are you ready to see your Daddy's nail skills?"

"Go ahead and eat first," she suggested, waving at the tray.

"I could eat every bite of those tamales, but I won't. Let me clean everything up and we'll get started."

"I can help," she offered.

"Nope. Daddy's job."

"Daddy has a tough life. He has to do everything," she joked.

"Daddies have a blessed life when they find their Littles. They get to care for her or him and make sure they're safe and happy. It is not a hardship. I love every second of having you in my life," Pedro assured her.

When she looked teary-eyed again, he added, "You can come sit at the counter and talk to me. We'll make that our beauty shop." He loved watching how the distraction helped her switch back to Belinda's normal joyful demeanor.

"I found a video. I couldn't do it myself. Especially for my right hand. My left hand doesn't like to hold the brush, much less draw a straight line."

"I can't wait to see it."

A few minutes later, Pedro had everything stored in the fridge and the dirty dishes placed in the dishwasher. "That's it. Show me what you found," he requested, sitting down on a stool next to her.

"You can tell me no," she assured him before hitting the play button.

A voice walked him through the stages as the technician decorated several nails in different colors. The final products were both super cute and professional. "I like this, Belinda. It's adorable and simple enough that I should be able to make it look—okay."

She laughed at his attempt to lower her expectations. "I think you'll do better than that. What do you think of these two colors together?"

"I like those." Pedro searched through the basket to find two other colors that complemented the first ones. "How about these for your pinkies?"

"I've seen people with different colors on their index fingers," she suggested.

"Little girls seem to need theirs on their pinkies. It's appropriate."

"Let's try it," she agreed with a nod. Belinda liked doing something just a hair different from others.

Pedro got to work. The pattern was easy. He painted each nail in half vertically with the two colors. The line between the shades was fairly straight, pleasing him. Calling the digital assistant's name, he requested high energy music.

116

A fast-paced song filled the room. "Time to dry those nails," he instructed, standing and helping her out of her chair.

Pedro launched into his trademarked fingernail drying dance moves he'd perfected over the years of doing his sisters' nails. The most basic move was shaking your hands through the air, but he'd become an expert at coordinating hip undulations and fancy footwork. Belinda's mouth dropped open as she watched.

"Come on, *mi corazón*. Dance with me."

Slowly, she took a few steps and wafted her nails through the air. Pedro moved behind her and pulled her back against his chest, tethering her lower body to his as he danced. Soon, Belinda relaxed against him and just let herself move. Laughter pealed from her lips as they danced together.

At the end of several songs, he called for the music to stop.

"Wait! We could keep going," she suggested with a hopeful expression.

"It's time for step two. Dots! Then more dancing," he promised.

Eagerly, she returned to her stool and held her hands out for him. Pedro had fun finishing the project. The final look turned out absolutely eye-catching. Each nail was two colors. For most, the right side was blue and the other purple. Then he'd plopped purple dots on the blue side and blue on the purple. Her pinkies were pale pink and lavender.

"I love them!" Belinda cooed as she displayed the final decorations in front of her.

"I do, too. You can coordinate all sorts of colors with them," he pointed out.

"You really do have sisters," she laughed.

"I do. They trained me well. I'm pretty good at helping cramps get better, too."

He watched her cheeks turn a rosy hue. "There are no secrets between a Daddy and his Little girl. You don't have to be embarrassed, *mi corazón*."

She nodded and then looked back at her nails. "Do we get to dance again?"

"That is the best way to get them dry." Pedro called for music and loved that she bounced out of her chair, ready to go. He joined her, wishing he could freeze this minute in time as her Little side didn't hesitate to enjoy herself. He was earning her trust.

* * *

"I THINK THEY'RE DRY," Belinda said sadly as she touched the top of one nail.

"We'll paint them again," he assured her.

"And dance?"

"Of course. There's no better way. Have some water and let's sit down on the couch to rest."

She drank deeply from the glass of water he handed her and couldn't stop looking at her nails. Belinda knew they would make her happy each time she looked at them. This had been such a fun evening. The best Friday night she'd had in a long time.

"Happy?" he asked.

Her gaze flew to his face. "So happy," she answered. "I love spending time with you. You're unlike anyone I've known before."

"I can live with that," he commented with a serious expression. "I know there's no one like you as well."

"We're pretty lucky," she suggested.

"Extremely. It's getting close to my baby girl's bedtime. Do you want to sleep here with Daddy or go back to your apartment?"

"Umm," she hummed and bit her lip. She really wanted to stay with him. "My apartment is lonely."

"Then you stay here with me and Tink."

"It's that easy?"

"It's that easy. Let's get you in the shower and then we'll go to bed."

"Aren't you going to shower with me?" she asked, batting her eyelashes as she remembered their previous shower experience.

"I'll be there to towel you off. If I get in the shower with you, it will be late before we sleep."

"It is the weekend," she suggested, trying not to be hurt by his refusal.

"Little girls need their sleep. We have two more days to enjoy each other. The first time we make love won't be when you're tired. I want you to remember everything."

A yawn stretched her mouth open and Belinda slapped a hand over it. "Sorry. I guess I am tired. It was a tough week," she admitted.

"Thank you for telling me the truth. Ready to shower?" he asked.

"Yes."

In twenty minutes, Belinda closed her eyes. She wore one of her Daddy's T-shirts, no panties, and held Bubbles. Pedro curled around her, breathing softly into her ear. The bed shifted a bit as Tinkerbell jumped up and found a comfy spot of his own at their feet. She felt her mouth curve in a smile. *This is heaven.*

CHAPTER 12

Purring woke her the next morning. Tinkerbell's inquisitive paw tapped her nose in a deliberate attempt to wake her. Belinda didn't want to leave the warm nest that snuggled around her. "Go away, kitty. I'll play later. Promise."

"Once he knows you're awake, he's going to pester you until you pet him," Pedro's low voice smoothed over her.

"He's spoiled, huh?"

"He's just a furry Little boy who knows what he wants," he teased. When he pressed stubbly kisses against her neck, she wiggled against him.

"Daddy, you need to shave!" Belinda protested as she scratched the sides of the cat's face.

"You don't like my whiskers? Let me show you how fun they can be." Pedro scooted backward as he rolled her over on her back. "Morning, *mi corazón!*"

Pedro kissed her deeply. His tongue swept into her mouth as she gasped in surprise. Belinda wove her fingers through his thick hair and held on as she tried to hold on to reality as he seduced her with sweet and demanding kisses. She never knew what to expect, but knew that she'd love it.

When he lifted his head, she rubbed a hand over the chafed skin around her mouth. "That's pokey. I don't see how that's fun."

"Daddy will show you."

Pedro lowered his mouth to kiss the hollow of her throat and pinched the front of her shirt at her waist. Pressing fiery kisses and small nibbles on her skin, he pulled the large T-shirt down, revealing her skin inch by inch as he tasted her. After a few preliminary kisses, Pedro pulled the neckline down to loop under her breast.

She opened her mouth to protest, but he captured her nipple between his lips and rolled it before sucking the peak into his mouth. Belinda arched her back to get closer to the sensation.

"No!" she protested when he lifted his head and released her nipple with a pop.

"I'm not finished here, Little girl. Just wait." He rubbed his chin lightly over the tip. His whiskers chafed her in a captivating way.

"Ooo." She'd never expected the bristles would feel so good. When he kissed the curve beneath her breast, Belinda closed her eyes at the sensation of his budding beard rasping over her skin.

"My Little girl likes a bit of pain with her pleasure," he purred against her skin.

Belinda shook her head quickly to refute that statement.

"Don't lie to Daddy," Pedro corrected her with a stern look that made her clench her thighs together as she remembered him spanking her.

"Let's get this shirt off," Pedro encouraged. He pulled the garment up her body and over her head, with Belinda curling up off the mattress to help him.

"Beautiful," he praised, looking over her body as he tossed the shirt somewhere in the room. He lowered his lips to her other breast to repeat his caresses on that side as well.

When he lifted his head, Pedro stroked down her body to rest his hand over her adult curls. "*Corazón*, would you like Daddy to make love to you?"

"Could you go slow?" she whispered, a grain of fear from the unknown lurking in the back of her brain.

"Baby girl, I wouldn't rush this for anything," he assured her. His solemn expression morphed into a slow wolfish grin that made her heart beat faster.

Suddenly, she wanted to see all that he could offer her. That small bit of fear of the unknown diminished as she focused on the magnetic man above her. Being brave, she braced herself on one elbow and wrapped a hand around his neck. "You'll teach me how to please you?"

"Oh, you please me, Little girl. We'll figure everything out together."

He slowly yielded to her gentle pressure to draw his mouth to hers. The anticipation gave her time to replay his words. They'd figure it out together. She liked that.

When his lips captured hers, Belinda put all her longing into that kiss. She wanted him to know how much he turned her on and that she'd only taken this step with him. His wordless response made her toes curl with excitement as he focused completely on her.

Drawing away, Pedro looked down at her. He brushed her hair from her face before placing kisses down her slender throat. She felt his touch sweep from her hip to cup her breast. One callused thumb brushed over her nipple as he created a trail of kisses ending at the sensitive underside of her breast. Belinda shivered as his tongue swept over it to reach his target. Now totally focused on the secondary sensation of his whiskers, she shivered underneath him as she lifted her pelvis toward him, willing him to stoke the fire already building between her thighs.

"Soon, Little girl," he promised her as he continued that steamy path of kisses and caresses until he braced himself on his elbows between her legs.

Belinda met his gaze as he looked over her body to her face. His eyes were dark and fiery with need.

"Watch us, *mi corazón*," he demanded.

When she nodded, Pedro lowered his mouth to her pussy. His groan of delight at her flavor made her lower her eyelids to savor the thrill of his enjoyment.

"Eyes on me!"

Batting her eyes open immediately, Belinda watched him lower his mouth to her once again. She struggled to keep her eyes focused on him as he cupped her hips and raised them to provide her with an angled view of her body and his play between her thighs. She could see him scoop up her slick juices on his tongue and nibble on her pink folds. Belinda didn't know why watching him made his touch incredibly arousing.

She could see the slick juices shining on her inner thighs as her body responded eagerly to his touch. His beard added a pinch of pain along with the thrilling sensations building within her. When he lowered her bottom to the bed, Belinda wrapped her fingers around the hard muscles of his shoulders and held on as he slid two fingers inside her. His fingers stroked the walls before scissoring open and closed to stretch her.

Struggling to keep watching, Belinda felt herself shaking as she watched him lavish pleasure on her. He divided his attention between looking at her and devouring her intimately with his gaze, as well as his mouth and fingers. When his lips sealed around her clit to suck it into his mouth, she bucked her hips upward as a cry burst from her lips.

Pedro didn't abandon his caresses. He simply gentled his touch to extend her pleasure as long as possible. When she had recovered, Belinda tugged at his shoulders. "Please. Please, Daddy. I need you inside me."

Pedro didn't make her ask twice. On all fours, he took a position over her. When Belinda stroked down his chiseled chest, he trapped her hands against his hard abdomen. "Do you wish to touch me?"

"Please," she asked before biting her bottom lip to keep herself from begging.

"All you need to do is ask for permission," he urged, frozen in place above her.

"Can I..." she started, but he interrupted.

"Daddy, may I..."

Belinda repeated his words and finished the request. "Daddy, may I touch your cock?"

"I would like that very much, Little girl," he said, and rewarded Belinda with a searing kiss that urged her to be brave. Lessening the pressure that held her hands against his stomach, Pedro guided them down his washboard abs to the tip of his shaft. He showed her how to wrap her hands around him and taught her the way he enjoyed being touched.

Under his tutelage, she raised her grip from the base to the top, drawing a heated groan from him in response. Feeling powerful, she repeated the process until he lunged forward to yank the nightstand drawer open.

"Temptress," he growled next to her ear after grabbing a condom from the drawer.

Pedro paused next to her, adding, "I can't wait any longer to be inside you, *mi corazón*. Are you ready to be one with Daddy?"

"Yes, Pedro. Please." She openly revealed her need for him.

"Can you call me Daddy, Little girl?"

She nodded with conviction. "Daddy, please," she repeated.

Pushing himself up to stand on his knees before her, Pedro quickly rolled the condom over his thick shaft. He pressed the broad head of his cock against her. "Take a deep breath, Belinda. Good. Now let it out and try to relax."

She followed his instructions and felt him glide forward into her. Air flooded back into her lungs when he stopped to allow her body to adjust to him. The slight sting of pain raised her arousal level. He fit inside her like a glove. Pedro wrapped his hands around her waist, holding her steady when she tried to lunge forward. Finally, dropping to one elbow next to her, Pedro slid fully inside her.

Belinda panted in reaction to his possession. He absolutely filled every millimeter of space inside her. She could feel his hot shaft inside her, pulsing with need. He wanted her as much as she did him. Belinda stroked his skin, feeling like the world around them had disappeared, leaving only them wrapped in each other's arms.

"Are you okay, *mi corazón*?" he whispered as he brushed her hair from her face.

"Move. I need you to move!"

With a chuckle, Pedro slid out of her and glided back inside. Her eyes almost rolled back in her head at the feeling. Pedro did not make her wait. He repeated the process until Belinda wrapped her arms and legs around him to hold him close.

"More!" she whispered.

That was the magic word. Pedro quickened his pace, driving into her. Their bodies became covered by a thin film of sweat as they strained together. Belinda could feel an orgasm growing inside her. She rubbed her pelvis against him and he shifted slightly.

"There," she whispered. Her fingernails bit into the muscles of his back. To her delight, his strokes focused on the tingling sensation as his hands explored every inch of her flesh. Belinda inhaled the heady scent of their desire.

She protested wordlessly when his hand slid between their gyrating bodies. His lips captured hers to distract her as his fingers stroked across her stomach and to her pussy. Pedro tapped on her clit. With a cry, the orgasm lurking over her burst.

Pounding into her, Pedro pushed himself to orgasm with her. He closed his teeth over her shoulder and bit into the tender skin. That pain fueled a new wave of pleasure inside her. "Daddy!"

In response, Pedro gathered her tenderly in his arms and rolled their bodies so she rested partially on top of him. Quickly, he dealt with the condom and held her close. His lips pressed against her temple. "So good, Little girl."

Belinda felt her lips curve as she closed her eyes, savoring his strength below her and the heat between her thighs as he stroked her back tenderly. His simple assessment summed everything up. Her life had flip-flopped upside down and back since he'd come to work at Edgewater Industries.

"Thank you for finding me," she whispered.

"I never would have stopped searching for you," he assured her, hugging her close.

Belinda could hear the truth ringing in his words. Once Pedro initiated a search, he would solve his quest.

CHAPTER 13

They were in the middle of eating a pile of pancakes cooked just as Belinda loved them—crispy on the edges and golden brown—when Pedro's phone rang.

He fed her another bite before reaching for the device and answering. "This is Pedro Morales."

"This is Easton, Pedro."

At the sound of her boss's voice, Belinda scooted off her Daddy's lap. She pressed her ear against the phone to listen.

"Save this number so you'll have it. We have a problem. All the doors in the cafeteria just slammed closed. There are people trapped inside. Security is trying to gain access, but the computer system is not allowing them to open those doors. Knox notified me and asked you and Belinda to come take a look."

"We're on our way. Give us five minutes. Where is he?"

"At the command center in the basement below Tower A."

"Got it."

Pedro disconnected the call. "Let me grab jeans and some sneakers. We'll dash to your room and get dressed. Grab your phone."

Responding immediately to the urgency in his voice, Belinda disconnected her phone from the charger and picked up his. She waited by the door for just a few seconds before her Daddy was back at her side.

He whisked her down the hallway to her apartment and inside when she opened it. Quickly, she pulled on jeans and an Edgewater polo before dropping to the floor in her closet to don her athletic shoes and tie them. Thank goodness they'd taken a shower after finally getting out of bed. She didn't want to show up smelling like sex. *My hair!*

Dashing into the bathroom, she tried to untangle the wild mess her hair had become. In her haste, she got the brush caught in the back. Tears welled in her eyes as she desperately tried to get it free.

"Little girl, I've got you," Pedro's voice smoothed over her, calming her panic. Deftly, he unwound the strands trapping the brush in place before taking over to smooth her hair. "Ponytail or down?"

She snagged a scrunchie from a basket on her vanity. "Ponytail, I think. Down is dangerous."

Belinda loved his chuckle as he secured her hair in a high ponytail where the blond strands would be out of the way. He kissed her exposed neck at the back before patting her on the bottom. "Call Daddy when you need him."

"Yes, sir," she agreed with a nod.

"Ready to go?"

"Let's get down there. I keep waiting for a second call to tell us everything is okay. It must be serious if Knox couldn't fix it," she commented.

Within a few minutes, they arrived where a small group of security people dressed in their official polos and others stood around a bank of computer screens and keyboards. Knox looked up from behind one keyboard. Concern lined his face as he met her gaze. Sharon hovered behind him.

"I'm glad to see you. The warning sensors went off at the security desk upstairs in building A. They called me immediately when they couldn't open the doors remotely or at the location. Soon after, people inside the cafeteria discovered that someone or something had locked them in. Calls flooded in. Easton has talked to them over the loudspeaker, explaining there's a minor glitch and we'll get them out soon. That calmed the panic." Knox detailed the situation quickly.

Immediately, Belinda knew he expected the atmosphere in the cafeteria to disintegrate again. "What have you discovered is happening electronically?"

"The computer system triggered the door locks at exactly nine o'clock," he answered.

"May I access the coding attached to the door system?" Pedro asked, moving around the desk.

"I just pulled it up for you," Knox confirmed, shifting out of his way.

Sharon, Fane, and Piper grouped together out of the way as they watched Pedro quickly typing in search functions. At times, different lines would flash a different color as he accessed the coding responsible for various aspects of controlling the door. After several minutes, Pedro looked up.

"What's happening mirrors the automatic response when a fire takes place. The doors would shut to close off the oxygen fueling the fire. People, however, still have the ability to push the door open manually to flee."

Knox nodded his agreement.

"How often is this coding updated?" Pedro asked, looking at Belinda.

"A piece of code like that? It was put in when the building opened. There would be no reason to touch it unless the doors were replaced or there was a problem with that server. Neither of those things has happened to the best of my knowledge since I started working here," she answered.

Easton shook his head as well. The CEO looked at Piper and Sharon. Both his current administrative assistant and his former one shook their heads, denying any information passing over their desks.

Pedro's expression became guarded. "Look at this piece of code I found. It was recently added to a program inside the cafeteria. It wasn't coded here at the tech hub or at the security desks. Someone added the code from a computer inside the cafeteria."

"The only computers in the cafeteria are the cash registers and the manager's laptop. We might have skilled coders working those positions, but I doubt it," Knox shared.

"As part of the on-boarding process for new hires, employees take a skills inventory survey. They solve problems and answer a ton of questions. That gives the human relations department insight into different positions they might have the skills to complete and enjoy," Sharon explained. As the corporate headhunter, she'd worked closely with HR.

"I didn't take that test," Pedro commented.

"We already knew you had skills," Belinda commented.

When the sexual undertone of her words registered and she realized how the others could misinterpret that line, Belinda added, "Finding that code that quickly is obvious proof that you've got programming mastered."

"That makes sense. So HR could provide us with the names of anyone with technical skills," he asked, thankfully not responding to her first statement.

"They could give us a list of people who might have the skills to do this," Sharon corrected. "I'll get on that immediately." She stepped away to make a phone call.

"I don't suppose it's as easy as taking out that one bit of code?" Easton's second-in-command, Elaine, asked, leaning forward to peer at the programing in front of her.

"No. I have a feeling that doing that will trigger something else. This appears to be part of a larger attack," Pedro replied, shaking his head in disbelief. "Whoever uploaded this coding didn't stop there. See the numbers at the end?"

"One of five," Elaine read. She looked up at Pedro. "You think five different attacks are going to happen?"

"The last is probably a ransom threat. That will demand Edgewater Industries pay an exorbitant amount of money to regain control," Pedro warned.

After letting those words sink in, Pedro added, "We can restore the system to the last backup before the assailant entered the attack into the computer. That will cause all business completed between that time and now to cease to exist and all records to be erased. All business transactions or interactions with the computer system will cease to exist. Edgewater Industries will lose everything that hasn't been backed up."

"Every morning at two-thirteen, the entire Edgewater Industries system automatically updates and creates a copy," Belinda informed them

"Losing over seven hours of business is going to make an impact. That's a drastic step," Easton concluded.

"If we do that, would we ever know who is responsible for this?" Sharon asked.

"No. We would also not know where the vulnerability is located that allowed them to launch an attack or if it's simply one employee trying to damage Edgewater Industries," Pedro sighed. "This isn't an act immediately or never do scenario. We could allow our people time to find and eliminate the threat. Then, we'll lose nothing and we'll have the evidence to convict the person who caused this."

"The sandbox!" Belinda chimed in.

When Pedro and Knox nodded, but everyone else looked at her blankly, she explained. "There is a testing area that programmers have nicknamed the sandbox. There they can design and change programming and monitor the effects to avoid causing system-wide problems during updates."

"If we have to restore the backup, we can copy all the evidence we have discovered and load it into the sandbox. It will remain there safely protected but not able to access Edgewater's systems and cause any harm."

"So, we have some time. We just need to stop it before we get to the fifth step. I'm presuming that would be the most catastrophic?"

Easton questioned, his quick mind already putting the pieces together.

"There's a risk there. I would assume the worst of this attack would come at the end, but it could happen at any time," Pedro said.

"I'm glad you're here, Pedro. I didn't build Edgewater Industries without taking some risks and creating a dedicated team of employees. I want to know who did this. Otherwise, we risk another attack."

With that decision made, the charismatic CEO looked around at the people he'd chosen as his inner circle. His eyes settled on Pedro. "What do you need?" Easton asked.

"A bank of laptops that we know are clean and the best coders you have available who you trust implicitly," Pedro answered, watching Belinda's expression as she immediately focused on the staffing component.

"How many computers do you want, Belinda?" Piper asked, pulling a number up on her phone.

"Get me ten. We'll start there," Belinda answered as she scrolled through her contacts. "Set them up in the open training area on the main floor by HR. I don't want any doors to trigger and make us lose access to them."

Pedro nodded his approval. There was no one else he'd want responsible for choosing people they could rely on.

"What can the rest of us do?" a large, tattooed man asked.

"Fane," Easton answered and inadvertently reminded Pedro of the man's name. "Could you and a couple of security guys head down to the cafeteria to muscle those doors off the hinges to free our people?"

"Of course," Fane agreed, as if glad to do something.

Pedro saw him pause to press his hand to the base of Elaine's back. When she looked at him, Pedro could see a silent message being transmitted. If he were correct, Fane was both Elaine's Daddy and her assistant. He'd just urged her to be careful. She nodded and Fane turned to leave. Their gazes intersected and Fane nodded, confirming all the conclusions Pedro had guessed.

"Tina Kaye, the hiring manager, is on her way in—about five minutes away. She left her computer on her desk. As soon as she accesses it, we'll have our list of those with possible coding skills," Sharon reported.

"Not Bill Weston?" Easton asked Sharon quietly.

When she shook her head, Easton added, "Then we need to make a staffing change." This time, his former administrative assistant agreed with a nod.

Pedro had met both Tina and Bill as he'd signed his hiring paperwork and completed the required training modules. It did not surprise him that in an emergency, Sharon would choose to work with the organized woman who accomplished so much with a smile. Bill, the head of HR, had only wished to impress Pedro since he was the special expert landed by Edgewater Industries. Although Pedro had not been in his new position for long, the leaders of most departments had already impressed him.

The response of the core team of employees impressed him. Pedro learned a lot about people when they were under pressure. No one here was panicking. Each contributed all they could to a team effort. Easton's focus was on the people, not his corporation. *This is a good place to be.*

"I'm heading to the training area. Do you want to come with me?" Belinda asked quietly.

"Let me know when your team is in place and you have a computer set up and ready for me to access it. Until then, I'll keep working here. I want to find that next point of attack before it happens."

"The elevators on all three floors just went offline," Knox reported.

He pulled his phone from his pocket and spoke clearly, "Code red, address anyone stuck in elevators first," before disconnecting.

Pedro knew they would soon be flooded with Knox's specially trained staff. His fingers flew over the coding to access anything that touched the elevators. This was tedious work. Despite the pressure they were under, he had to be meticulous.

"How many minutes between the first and second event?" he asked Knox who worked next to him.

"Ninety minutes. The doors triggered at nine. It's now ten-thirty," Knox reported, making himself notes.

"If the pattern continues—noon, one-thirty, and three," Pedro projected.

"I'll pull up our emergency plan," Easton said quietly. "We'll be ready for whatever happens."

CHAPTER 14

"I found something," an excited voice called, pulling everyone's attention from their computers.

"It looks like the next target is going to be..."

A rumble of quiet clicks that alone would have been overlooked, but layered on top of each other created a sound like thunder rolled throughout the building.

"...the doors," the programmer finished his sentence. "I was so close. Sorry. I just didn't find it quickly enough."

Pedro called Knox. "We just lost the door locks everywhere. If there are any sensitive or financial items behind a locked door—any kind of locked door—you'll need to secure it."

"On it. Vaults first," Knox announced, letting Pedro know he understood the message.

"Tinkerbell!" Belinda whispered into his ear. "He'll be loose. I'll go figure out how to keep him safe in your apartment."

"Tinkerbell is fine. He'll find a place to hide and sleep in the apartment until we get back. He's not really the adventurous type."

"He goes back and forth across the balconies, and we're on the seventh floor," Belinda protested.

"Oh, he's ornery and a daredevil, but shy. He visits you only because he is as attracted to you as I am," Pedro assured her quietly. He loved the blush that tinted her cheeks.

"Pedro, you remember Tina. She just sent you the list of employees scoring high in tech skills on the inventory test. Only one is on staff today and in the cafeteria," Sharon said, shaking her head as if she couldn't believe it.

"I need to talk to her," Pedro said urgently.

"Knox has gone to get her. He looked very focused, like he knew something but hadn't connected the pieces. She's set up a sandwich making station outside the building and is creating picnics for anyone that's hungry."

That did not sound like a disgruntled employee who would attack the computer systems. "Who is it?" Pedro asked Tina and Sharon.

"Cynthia Grant," Sharon answered, shaking her head. "We've notified Knox, but there has to be some other person who snuck in."

That name triggered Pedro's memory. He waved a hand to get Belinda's attention. "Cynthia Grant," he said when she was close.

"Cynthia." Belinda's face fell. "She was so upset on Thursday. She left after we talked but was back in the cafeteria yesterday. I asked if everything was okay. She smiled and apologized for making a scene before excusing herself to help in the kitchen."

"She's gone," Knox said, jogging into the room to join the group gathered around Pedro's computer. "I'll go notify Easton. Tina, can you send me Cynthia's address, phone number, and emergency contacts?"

"We'll get started looking for anything that has Cynthia's touch. We've seen three sets of code now," Pedro shared before calling the programmers to the middle of the room.

Belinda followed him and stood at the edge of the group. She loved how the group had immediately recognized Pedro's expertise and followed his instructions without branching out on their own. Coders were a solitary breed, and each had their own style.

"Belinda, would you put the three lines of code on big display for us to look at?" he asked, and she rushed away to make it happen.

Sixty seconds later, she was back. "The display is coming online," she reported.

"Thank you, Belinda."

Pedro turned to look at the coding. "We can identify these pieces of code as being added this morning. Each has similarities. We know there is a countdown." Pedro pointed to the symbols in the corner signaling one slash five, two slash five, and three slash five.

"I've tried searching for those symbols or for the others we expect are coming. I'm not finding it. What do you see?" he asked the assembled employees.

"It doesn't follow the coding language exactly. There's something added into each one, as if they didn't know our system perfectly or they're not trained," one woman pointed out.

"I see that, too." The others nodded their agreement and Pedro continued. "Does that give us anything searchable?"

"Each one has those forward slashes. We use those to put notes into programs we're building as documentation. There would be millions of those to search for," another programmer suggested.

"There aren't any notes in the area she added between the slashes except a few random letters."

Knox picked up a marker and a whiteboard Sharon had brought in. "Read the letters for me in the first three."

Quickly, he jotted them down as Pedro read them: HEMAD.

"He mad?" Knox read aloud.

"I think you'd have to be pissed to do this to a company you work for," Sharon suggested.

"No. There's more coming." Belinda ran to the whiteboard and held her hand out for the marker. "That's not what Cynthia said." She added three more letters to the board: E, M, E.

The group read, "He made me."

"That's it. Look for those next letters in conjunction with the forward slashes," Pedro ordered.

Everyone flew back to their computers as he checked the time. One o'clock. They had thirty minutes. Peering into his computer, he joined the search.

Ten minutes later, Belinda shouted, "I've got it! The financial centers are next. The code is sending everything to an account code."

"Good job, Belinda. Copy everything up to this point and dump it into the sandbox." Pedro praised her, being careful to use her name and not Little girl. There wasn't time to remove all traces of the coding. They'd have to use the backup.

Immediately, she got busy. He watched her fingers fly across the keys with complete confidence that she had this.

"We need Easton, now."

Four minutes later, he jogged into the room, out of breath. "Sorry. I was helping at the gate. We've stationed all the security teams at vital places."

"It's time to put the backup in place. We found the code but can't remove it entirely with all confidence," Pedro told him.

"What's the next attack?" Easton asked.

"The Edgewater financial centers are all targeted at transferring the funds to an account somewhere," Pedro answered.

"Do we have time to get the back up going and preserve the evidence?" Easton asked.

"Done," Belinda announced.

"Everything is in the sandbox now, sir. We just need your authorization code," Pedro informed him. "You do understand that you will lose a lot of money and information by dumping everything that happened from two-thirteen until now—almost twelve hours."

"Show me where to type in my code," Easton requested. He didn't hesitate or show any concern.

"I set it up on this computer—just in case, sir."

CHAPTER 15

In the days following the attack, Belinda raced from meeting to meeting to put out fires after they put the backup in place. Vigilant employees, at different sites already working on the next business day, had documented their activities. That assisted the process of reestablishing what had been wiped out.

When she had a moment free, Belinda thought of the young woman who was now a fugitive from the police and several other government agencies. No one could believe that Cynthia had masterminded this. Unfortunately, the longer she evaded capture, the guiltier she appeared.

Belinda scheduled a quick fifteen-minute meeting with Easton to tell him of her conversation with Cynthia.

"She wanted me to tell you she didn't do this vindictively. That someone was forcing her to do it. And that she was sorry," Belinda told her boss.

"You reported this to someone?" Easton asked sharply.

"Immediately, sir. I described the encounter to Knox, and he started investigating. I got the impression from her words and actions that she felt threatened by someone she knew well."

Easton shook his head. "She's disappeared. That makes her look more guilty."

Belinda shrugged. "I wish I could go back and talk to her again. Maybe there was something I could have said to prevent this."

"Thank you for coming to talk to me, Belinda. We both know that if someone wishes to act in bad faith, there is very little someone can do to deter them."

"Of everything she said, Cynthia emphasized she wanted to me tell you she didn't have another option."

"When she is found, I'll keep that in mind."

* * *

BELINDA COULDN'T SAY the exact day when her Daddy moved in with her. From the beginning of their relationship, his focus on her and willingness to work through the roadblocks she placed in their way had proven that she topped his priority list. He simply wanted to be with her as much as possible. They spent time together doing all the activities that Belinda had dreamed of doing as she'd read those books and fantasized of having a Daddy of her own. Only now, Pedro read those stories to her at bedtime—only one chapter at a time so she could get enough sleep before the next busy day. Much to her delight if that chapter made her wiggle too much with excitement, he could always find a way to exhaust her.

Last night, she'd asked to color in one of the new activity books he'd purchased for her. Sitting on his lap, she'd carefully looked through the pages to find her favorite one to start with. She felt a bit silly focusing on coloring while he watched.

"Can you choose a picture for me to decorate, too?" Pedro asked, looking over the pages as she thumbed through them.

Peeking up at him, she asked, "You're going to color, Daddy?"

"I thought I'd see if I can stay inside the lines. It's been a long time since I used crayons. You won't laugh at me, will you, *mi corazón?*"

"No way," she'd assured him and then had deliberately chosen a fairly simple page for him to work on. "How about this one?"

"I love it. I think I'll make the butterfly orange like those ones we saw in the greenspace yesterday," he announced.

"That will be beautiful, Daddy. Maybe with black antennae?" she suggested as they settled close together on the floor to share crayons.

She'd been so good and hadn't giggled once when he said "Oops!" He'd promised they could finish tonight after dinner. Belinda had looked forward to it all day. Now finally, she turned the corner toward her apartment after another busy day in the position she loved so much. A late conference with Easton had delayed her and she'd missed walking home with Pedro.

Opening her door, Belinda paused in the doorway to sniff. "You're making spaghetti?" she called. "Tell me there are meatballs and I'll beg."

"Oh, you'll beg," Pedro answered in his low, sexy voice as he emerged from the kitchen. His path past the refrigerator ruffled the pages still attached. Reminding her of that phrase, he'd made sure she wouldn't forget. His daily actions underlined the truth contained in that simple phrase. Her Daddy only wanted the best for her.

Her eyes shifted from the rustling pages to focus on his appearance. Belinda couldn't stop laughter from spilling from her lips. The pink frilly apron that Pedro wore strained to cover his bare chest. Quickly, she took a picture.

"Private use only," he reprimanded her.

"Could I show it to my mom? I know she never imagined it would look so good," Belinda asked, holding a hand to her belly as she laughed.

"So, you're going to tell your family about me?" he asked, instantly detouring the funny situation to a much more important discussion.

"Yes?" she answered, shrugging her shoulders and trying to act cool. Belinda didn't want him to think she was pushing for more than he wanted to give too soon. "I mean, I don't have a plan or dates, but I want to you meet my family someday."

"Mine are coming in two weeks. They are going to stay in my apartment," he informed her as he stepped closer to wrap his arms around her.

"All your family?" she asked, remembering the picture he'd shown her.

"My youngest two sisters are hugely pregnant. According to Mom, they aren't traveling now. It will just be my mom, my dad, and my sister and brother who are closest in age to me. Oh, and my brother's family."

"All those people can't fit in your apartment with you," Belinda protested.

"I'm staying here with you. Knox got permission for me to use the apartment on the other side of the hall as well. It has two bedrooms. That will give us plenty of room."

She stared at him, trying to figure out what to say. "Mmm, that's a lot of people. And you're going to stay here? What will your parents say?"

"How glad they are to meet you and welcome to the family," Pedro told her with a smile.

"But I'm not really part of the family. I'm just your girlfriend."

"That's not correct," he answered with a dangerous glint reflecting in his eyes.

Belinda had already learned to pay attention when she saw that look. "I mean, I'm your girlfriend. The one they've never met. You haven't been here for too long. I'm sure in their eyes our relationship couldn't be serious."

Pedro cupped the back of her head and tightened his arm around her, pulling her forward until their bodies pressed tightly together. His mouth descended over hers and he kissed her with the skill that always distracted her from anything else. When they were both breathing heavily, he leaned his forehead against hers to give them a moment to recover.

After a few seconds, he lifted his head to look deep into her eyes. "You aren't my girlfriend. You're my Little girl."

He hasn't told them that, has he?

When she panicked and pushed away, he quickly clarified, "No, they don't know that you're a Little. Our private business is only ours.

148

Do I know my brother who'll visit is a Daddy? Yes. We sympathized with each other during our searches. Do I know without being told that my oldest sister is a Little girl? Yes."

"You haven't told them I'm Little?" she asked skeptically.

"I have not. My fidelity goes to you only, *mi corazón*. I will protect you before anyone else," he vowed.

"Really? I know how important your family is to you. I don't want to get in the way," she whispered.

"They will love you as much as I do."

"You love me?" she repeated before she could stop herself. Her gaze dropped to the lace around the top of the frilly apron. She didn't want to see him search for a way out of the box she'd trapped him in.

"I mean, I know it's too fast to love me. But you care about me?" she asked, peeking up at him before dropping her focus again to that lacy edge.

His fingers cupped her chin and tilted her head until their eyes focused on each other. "I love you, Little girl, *mi corazón*, Belinda. I will love you today, tomorrow, and all the days after that."

"Really?" she asked, feeling tears tumble from her eyes and spill over her cheeks.

"Truly." He placed her hand under the frilly top of the apron, pressing it against his warm skin over his strong heartbeat. "You have my heart forever."

Belinda stared at her hand tucked under the fabric. Bravely, she met his gaze with her own. Stiffening her spine, she whispered, "I've never felt like this, Pedro. I want to be with you every moment of the day and night. I think so much of you both personally and professionally. You are the exact person I've been searching for all my life. I keep waiting to screw this up."

"You will screw something up and a punishment will wipe it away." He patted her bottom fondly. "I'll make mistakes, too, even though I'll try to be the best Daddy I can."

"Do I get to spank you?" she asked, grinning at that thought.

"No. Spanking is for naughty Little girls or boys. Serious conversations are for Daddies who screw something up. I'll create a stuffie, chocolate, and flower fund to help me apologize."

"I like chocolate," she whispered.

"I know. You've eaten all my treats from the bottom drawer in my desk," he teased.

"Sorry?"

"No apologies needed for coming to see me and stocking up on energy to make it through your day. I'm glad I'm the one you want to recover with," he said softly.

She stepped close again to hug him and he squeezed her against his hard body as if savoring the feel of her. Belinda closed her eyes and laid her head on his chest. Pedro had become her sanctuary. She almost purred when his hand unfastened her ponytail and his fingers combed through her hair, massaging her scalp.

"You're going to marry me when you're ready or six months from now, whichever happens first. Then, we'll create our own brood of brothers and sisters who alternatively love and hate each other."

"We're going to get married in six months?" she repeated, leaning away from his body to search his face.

"Unless you have something else happening on January first." Pedro arched one questioning eyebrow.

"We're getting married on January first?" she repeated, trying to sort out all the information he had surprised her with.

"Yes. I like that date. It's my birthday."

"You want to get married on your birthday?" she double-checked.

"You are the best present I could ever receive," he shared with an indulgent smile.

"Do I get any say in this?" she laughed. *Surely, he's joking.*

"Sure, when's your birthday?"

"September thirteenth."

"That works, too. We could get married on September thirteenth," Pedro agreed, moving up the timeline for their wedding.

"That's only a few weeks away," she panicked.

"Better to wait until January first, hmmm?" he asked.

When she nodded, he concluded, "Perfect. January first, you will become Mrs. Pedro Morales."

He took a step back and lowered himself to kneel on one knee. "I talked to your father this morning. Your parents have given me their blessing."

She shook her head in disbelief at all the information she tried to understand and assimilate into her brain. "You called my father?"

He winked and reached out to take her hand. "I love you, Little girl. Now shush, and let me do this right."

Taking a deep breath, Pedro asked, "Belinda Marie Jenkins, will you be my bride and forever my Little to hold and treasure for all the time we have left in this world?"

"Daddy? You're not teasing me, are you?"

"No, *mi corazón*. I am very serious." He squeezed her hand to reassure her.

"Oh, I forgot something." Pedro reached into his pocket and retrieved a small velvet box. Opening it, he revealed a gorgeous red ruby surrounded by sparkling diamonds with a matching wedding ring wrapped around the dazzling center stones.

"That's the ring you selected for me? People are going to chop my finger off to steal it," she said before she could stop herself. Belinda stretched out a hand to stroke her finger over the unbelievable display of sparkling stones.

"No one is removing your finger, Little girl. If you don't like it, we can choose another," he suggested, watching her face.

"Oh, no. I love it. It's the loveliest thing I've ever seen."

"What do you think, Little girl? January first?"

"January first sounds perfect," she answered in a rush of words.

"That's my girl," he praised as he stood agilely to take her hand. "I'll take out the engagement ring for now. Let's see if it fits."

Pedro slid the ring over her knuckle and into place. "Perfect."

She held her hand out to admire the gorgeous ring. It matched the nails that her Daddy had refreshed just the night before—glitter white polish with a red heart addition at the tip. He'd planned this.

"You could have told me last night," she whispered.

"That was my plan, but you spent time in the corner with your naughty plug in place," he reminded her softly.

"Daddy!" she protested, feeling her cheeks heat. Belinda still regretted snapping at her Daddy because she'd had such a grueling day.

"There is no one here but you and me, *mi corazón*, and we both know you needed corner time."

"No more. I'll be good," she promised.

"Thankfully, the corners will remain in whatever house we own. And the plug? You wore the smallest size in the case. There are plenty more to keep you company while you think. I did get you this as well."

Pedro shifted the frilly apron to reveal the other side pocket and pulled out a thick plug with a jeweled top, complete with a red heart. "You can wear this as you walk down the aisle to help remind you who you belong to."

"That's too big."

"By January, you'll be ready to wear it. Nothing will be off limits between the two of us. Perhaps we'll set a goal of having me make love to your bottom on our wedding night."

She squeezed her thighs together, willing herself not to react to his words. Her panties were already soaked. Holding the heavy plug in her hand should scare her, but instead, she was completely turned on, imagining the sting of her bottom as he pressed it into place before she walked down the aisle to become his. The idea of a private reminder between Daddy and Little girl thrilled her.

His thumb brushed over one erect nipple, pushing against the padding of her bra. "Your body says yes. What does your heart say?"

"Yes, Daddy."

With a roar, Pedro wrapped his arms around her and swept her feet from the floor. Turning in a tight circle, he celebrated her acquiescence. "I love you, Little girl."

"I love you, too, Daddy," she answered truthfully, realizing a million days wouldn't have been enough time for her to decide anyone else was her perfect match. Two weeks and video conferences before they'd met were more than enough for her to know that Pedro was her one. *My Daddy.*

Pedro let her slide down the front of his body, allowing her to feel his arousal. "By the way, your mom and dad are coming to meet me the week after my side of the family is here. They can stay at my apartment."

"What?"

"You're not hungry, right?" he asked, guiding her into the kitchen, where he turned off the flame under the bubbling sauce.

"I could be," she commented, trying to figure out where this conversation was headed now.

"Exactly what I thought. You need to relax before dinner." Pedro carefully unfastened the borrowed apron and placed it on the counter.

Crowding Belinda against the blank wall, he unfastened her slacks and pushed them over her hips to let them settle on the floor. "I like these," he commented, tracing the white lace edging on the red heart thong he'd dressed her in that morning.

"You chose those on purpose," she said with a gasp, having forgotten what she wore.

"Guilty. They look so good on you." He looped his finger under the thin strap that ran between her buttocks. Pedro pulled up on this string gently, rubbing the fabric over that small hidden opening.

"But, *mi corazón*, these panties have become totally soaked. They need to come off."

"It's your fault," she whispered and looked down at the plug still resting in her hand.

"You are going to love taking me deep inside your bottom. For now, I think you need a quick release." He pulled the panties down to her ankles and helped her step out of her clothing.

"Turn around, Little girl," Pedro requested, turning his finger in a circle.

She slowly complied and looked over her shoulder. *He isn't going to...*

"Hands on the wall."

"Should I take off my shoes?" Belinda offered, drawing his attention to her stilettos.

"When we're done," Pedro assured her as he unfastened his pants and pushed them over his hips.

She heard the rustle of the condom and knew he protected her. His arm encircled her waist, pulling her hips back to him. Belinda kept her hands plastered to the wall, or as best she could, while holding the plug in her palm. Lifting her bottom to present herself to him, Belinda held her breath as he fit the broad head of his cock to her opening. With one powerful thrust, he filled her, pushing all the air from her lungs.

"Do you wish to beg?" he asked, playfully reminding her of their conversation as she'd walked in the door.

"Please, Daddy. Make me come."

"My pleasure, *mi corazón.*"

His skilled thrusts pushed her arousal high quickly. The promises contained in his sweet caresses assured her he wouldn't stop until he'd erased the long day completely from her mind. Rule one popped into her mind. *No talk about work after hours.*

She loved being a Little girl.

No, Belinda corrected herself. She loved being *his* Little girl.

She peeked over her shoulder at him when he plucked the plug from her gripping hand.

"Daddy's toy."

Belinda shivered as he used its tip to draw a line slowly down the center of her torso. He marked her newly shaven mound with an X. The flesh was so sensitive that she clenched tightly around his cock deep inside her, drawing an appreciative moan from his lips against her ear. Pedro traced the line of her cleft and pressed the plug into her pink folds. She gasped as he rubbed it against her clit, making her wobble on her high heels as she struggled for balance.

"You're going to love this plug, Little girl," he whispered into her ear.

She nodded emphatically in agreement before pressing one cheek to the cold paint as his other hand drew her attention from the stroking plug. Pedro removed his supportive arm from around her waist to stroke his thumb between her buttocks. Belinda froze against the wall as he pressed against that small opening her gift was designed to fill.

"Daddy's going to prepare you to take him here, *mi corazón*. Are you going to be a good girl for me?"

"Yes, yes, yes!" she screamed against the wall as the first orgasm hit.

CHAPTER 16

Easton looked across the table at his chief legal counsel in the dimly lit, wood-paneled bar. He always enjoyed meeting his college friend here for their monthly conversations. The rule had always been to focus on anything but business. Easton was prepared to break that agreement today.

"I need you to prove that she's innocent, Dirk."

"I've looked at the file, Easton. I won't sugarcoat this for you. I don't know if I can get her off. Every single path seems to point to her working alone," Dirk told him with a shake of his head before lifting the cut-glass tumbler of amber scotch.

"She's a Little. She needs someone in her corner. I don't believe she did this," Easton informed him.

"This isn't the type of law I specialize in, Easton. She would do better with a criminal attorney to protect her in the courtroom. I can suggest a few highly skilled trial lawyers..."

Easton shook his head and interrupted. "She's coming to you. I want you to handle this."

"Because you think she's innocent?" Dirk suggested.

"Because I know she's innocent and I don't want whoever forced her to do this to ruin her life. I have a feeling he's had a hand in screwing up her success before."

"That's a big hunch to risk letting someone who almost transferred all your money to an offshore account get away with betraying your company. She would have hurt many more people than just you," Dirk pointed out.

"I'm aware of that. I'm calling in my favor," Easton said softly.

Dirk blinked at him in surprise. "Really? You're going to use your favor to have me defend this woman?"

"I'm going to use my favor to have you prove her innocence," Easton clarified, before glancing at his watch. "Cynthia is turning herself in to you this evening."

"Did you just say she's turning herself in to me?" Dirk asked, focusing on Easton's exact words.

"Yes. You'll find her under the stairs of your deck. I told her she would be safe there until I convinced you to represent her."

"No judge is going to allow me to represent both the company and the person accused of trying to steal billions of dollars from that company," Dirk pointed out.

"So, for once, you don't represent me. Choose an assistant legal counsel to take your place. A good one. I don't want there to be any question that she had a fair trial and has been completely cleared," Easton instructed.

"This isn't a sound business decision, Easton," Dirk warned. "I would like you to think about this over a week or two before you make your final choice of how to proceed."

"I appreciate your counsel, Dirk. You are my oldest friend and the one who's guided me to establish all that Edgewater Industries has become. I assure you, I'm not going into this blindly."

"When I find her hiding under my deck, I will have to take her to the police station to turn herself in," Dirk said firmly. "I can't harbor an alleged felon."

"Take time to talk to her, Dirk. Surely a few hours of conversation between a lawyer and his client would be normal before you escort her to the authorities?"

"That would not be uncommon," Dirk allowed, setting his full glass down on the table with a quiet thump.

"Thank you, my friend," Easton said, recognizing that Dirk had decided to take the case and wanted to stay clear-headed.

"You're going to owe me several of these when this is all done," Dirk warned.

"I will look forward to celebrating with you." Easton signaled for the bill as Dirk pushed his chair back from the table.

"It's getting ready to rain. I wouldn't want a stray dog to struggle to stay dry under my deck. I'll be in touch," he promised.

"She deserves your best," Easton said quietly.

"I wouldn't give her anything less," Dirk assured him before leaving.

Easton sampled the fine scotch in his glass and smiled. His friend had no idea what he was walking into. Damn, this would be fun to watch.

He sent the server off to charge his credit card and messaged Piper. "On my way home. Everything is set."

The return message made him smile. A line of alternating Xs and Os filled several lines of text. His Little girl had needed him badly in the beginning as well. He hoped Dirk garnered as much happiness as Easton had found with Piper.

CHAPTER 17

Belinda was sure that none of the kitchens in the Edgewater apartments had ever held as many people as currently stood in Pedro's. She watched carefully as Pedro's mother, Sara, demonstrated the correct method of making a tamale. Determined, she picked up a corn husk and placed it flat on her hand.

Giving her support, Pedro's sisters and sister-in-law mirrored her action. Two stood on either side of her while the two expectant mothers had joined through a computer link. Belinda spread a layer of the cornmeal mixture everyone called masa on the damp husk, adding a bit more when Sara offered her a partially filled spoon. She added a row of cooked chicken down the middle and carefully wrapped the bottom and sides together before tying it together with a strip of husk.

"Does that look right?" Belinda asked hesitantly, as she held it out on her palm.

Everyone fell silent as Sara plucked it from her hand. The matron of this closely knit clan examined it thoroughly and weighed its heaviness on her palm. After several long seconds, she looked up to meet Belinda's gaze. "Absolutely perfect. I guess we can officially consider you part of the family now."

A roar of excited chatter and congratulations rolled in from all sides of Belinda as everyone seemed to hug her at once. Sagging in relief, Belinda picked up her margarita that seemed to be the traditional drink for the Morales women while creating tamales and took a long drink. As everyone celebrated around her, she toasted the smiling women on the screen.

"My tamale was the worst you've ever seen, wasn't it?" Belinda guessed.

"Oh, no. You should have seen Mariana's first. It split through the cornhusk and crumbled to the floor. Yours stayed in a tamale shape," Helena congratulated.

"Yours was excellent," Sara reassured her, wrapping an arm around Belinda's waist to hug her close. She waved a warning finger at her daughter on screen who had spilled the beans.

"You will have many years to make tamales with us. In a few years, we will help you teach your daughters how to make them as well," Pedro's mother informed her.

"How many children are you expecting?" Belinda blurted.

"As many or as few as the two of you decide. There is no pressure from us for you to have a family. We are perfectly content now that we can see how happy Pedro is and how ideal you are for each other."

"Exactly, *mamá*," her daughters echoed.

"I never had any siblings. Or a mom who cooked," Belinda confessed.

"You are going to get so tired of us," Mariana teased through the screen.

"Never. We'll just send you home after the tamales are made," Pedro informed them from the doorway. His gaze met Belinda's, obviously checking to make sure she was doing okay with his family.

"Take your bride to be away and give her kisses. Then bring her back so we can tell her all the embarrassing stories of you as a kid," Sara directed and shooed them from the kitchen.

Pedro quickly led her out of his apartment to the quiet of their bedroom in hers. Tinkerbell was curled up on the pillows, wrapped around Bubbles with his face propped on the platypus's beak.

"Looks like Tink chose to have some alone time."

She looked around at the small things he'd included to take care of her as his Little girl. A soft blanket lay on the chest at the end of the bed. She'd learned to enjoy the naps he scheduled for her on the weekends. The basket of small rewards nestled on her dresser. She loved earning stickers or fancy coloring books and crayons for being good. Pedro showed her every day how to enjoy being true to the Little girl inside her.

He wrapped his arms around her. "Need to escape?" he asked.

"No. I'm having fun. I like your family. They're loud and fun. I think they like me," she hesitantly suggested.

"I know they love you. My mom is showing you how to make tamales. That usually doesn't happen until you produce a grandchild," Pedro laughed.

"Do you think they'll be unhappy when we wait a few years before trying to have a child?" Belinda asked.

"No. I think my parents had despaired that I'd ever find the one I searched for. *Mamá* shared frequently that I was too picky and warned that I would end up sad and alone. They've changed their minds after meeting you."

"I'm glad you found me, too, Daddy."

Pedro rewarded her with several kisses before giving her a squeeze. When his phone rang, he pulled it from his pocket and answered. "*Sí, mamá.*"

He laughed into the receiver before pushing the button to let her hear. "The tamales are calling," he joked. "Listen."

"What?" Belinda strained to hear.

"Tamales! Tamales! Tamales!" drifted through the phone.

"The tamales are calling?" she laughed.

"The Morales clan always heeds the call of the tamales," he joked. "Would you make some spicy ones for me?"

"Bring me another margarita and I'll make sure to pepper a few up for you," Belinda suggested.

"Deal!" he agreed. The loving look in his eyes reassured her completely that her Daddy was the one she'd dreamed of as hard as he had searched for her.

* * *

Thank you for reading Daddy's Searching! If you enjoyed this story you'll won't want to miss the next one, Daddy's Protecting. Preorder yours today!

Don't miss future sweet and steamy Daddy stories by Pepper North? Subscribe to my newsletter!

Read more from Pepper North!

Dr. Richards' Littles®

A beloved age play series that features Littles who find their forever
Daddies and Mommies. Dr. Richards guides and supports their efforts
to keep their Littles happy and healthy.
Available on Amazon

Dr. Richards' Littles®
is a registered trademark of
With A Wink Publishing, LLC.
All rights reserved.

SANCTUM

Pepper North introduces you to an age play community that is isolated from the surrounding world. Here Littles can be Little, and Daddies can care for their Littles and keep them protected from the outside world.

Available on Amazon

Soldier Daddies

What private mission are these elite soldiers undertaking? They're all
searching for their perfect Little girl.
Available on Amazon

The Keepers

This series from Pepper North is a twist on contemporary age play romances. Here are the stories of humans cared for by specially selected Keepers of an alien race. These are science fiction novels that age play readers will love!
Available on Amazon

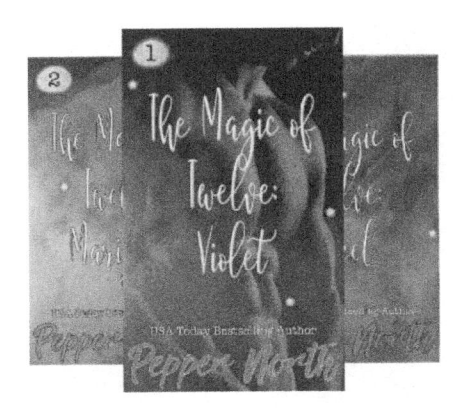

The Magic of Twelve

The Magic of Twelve features the stories of twelve women transported on their 22nd birthday to a new life as the droblin (cherished Little one) of a Sorcerer of Bairn. These magic wielders have waited a long time to take complete care of their droblin's needs. They will protect their precious one to their last drop of magic from a growing menace. Each novel is a complete story.

Available on Amazon

Ever just gone for it? That's what *USA Today* Bestselling Author Pepper North did in 2017 when she posted a book for sale on Amazon without telling anyone. Thanks to her amazing fans, the support of the writing community, Mr. North, and a killer schedule, she has now written more than 80 books!
Enjoy contemporary, paranormal, dark, and erotic romances that are both sweet and steamy? Pepper will convert you into one of her loyal readers. What's coming in the future? A Daddypalooza!

Sign up for Pepper North's newsletter

Like Pepper North on Facebook

Join Pepper's Readers' Group for insider information and giveaways!

Follow Pepper everywhere!

Amazon Author Page
BookBub
FaceBook
GoodReads
Instagram
TikToc
Twitter
YouTube
Visit Pepper's website for a current checklist of books!

Made in the USA
Monee, IL
12 August 2022

11496268R00098